The boy was laughably small. Remo watched as the youth pulled boxes off shelves and over-turned display cases of baseball bats and sports equipment.

"Sloppy," Remo said.

Sparky spun around. "What do you want?" he said.

"I'm putting the damper on you tonight, kid." Remo said.

He took a step forward, then stopped. The boy had raised his arms out to his sides, as if he were doing a Dracula impersonation at a backyard carnival.

Then, before Remo's eyes, the boy began to glow. A blue aura surrounded his frail body. As Remo watched, the colors began to change . . . to purple, to red, to orange, to a brilliant, fiery yellow, and then as Remo moved across the floor toward him, Sparky pointed his hands at Remo, and splashes of flame flew across the room. Remo slid sideways, but he felt the flame brush his clothing. It was burning. He was burning. He dropped to the floor and rolled, trying to put out the fire. The heat seared his face. There was a smell, too. A bittersweet smell of roast pork, and then Remo realized it was the smell of his flesh where he had been burned. Again he rolled along the floor, putting the fire out, and with a growl, jumped over the counter and ran to the open door. Sparky was getting into a car across the street. The man behind the wheel saw Remo coming and quickly threw the car into gear. Remo knew he could reach the car before it got away.

And then behind him, he heard it.

A scream . . .

THE DESTROYER SERIES:

The Destroyer 41

Warren Murphy

FIRING LINE

PINNACLE BOOKS   LOS ANGELES

THE DESTROYER #41: FIRING LINE

Copyright © 1980 by Richard Sapir and Warren Murphy

An original Pinnacle Books edition, published for the first time anywhere.

First printing, August 1980

ISBN: 0-523-40715-7

Cover illustration by Hector Garrido

Printed in the United States of America

PINNACLE BOOKS, INC.
2029 Century Park East
Los Angeles, California 90067

FIRING LINE

CHAPTER ONE

Solly Martin had a theory that great ideas are diamonds, not pearls. By which he meant that great ideas spring up full-blown in flashes of inspiration; they are not created, as a pearl is created, by layer after layer of idea and change and improvement, until one day a piece of sand has been converted into something brilliant and pure.

So it surprised Solly that when he had his great idea—to burn down America—it had not come on him all at once, but had been carefully built in his mind from the first irritating sand-speck of a thought.

Solly Martin was a businessman, although when he told this to his Uncle Nathan who was visiting his sister, Solly's mother, in Coney Island, Uncle Nathan had said to his sister, as if Solly were not in the room, "If this is a businessman, I am the Pope of Rome."

Solly did not like his Uncle Nathan; the old man had yellow teeth, chewed with his mouth open and had a craving for kreplach that bordered on the unnatural, and the abolition of kreplach from the house had been Solly's first manly demand upon reaching the age of puberty and being bar mitzvahed.

2

"You'll see, Uncle Nathan," Solly had said.

Uncle Nathan buried his face in the dish of Jewish dumplings. "Just so he doesn't go asking me to invest any money," he said to Solly's mother. "Some businessman. Already starting to go bald, and still to earn his first smart dollar. It is to laugh."

Solly shrugged off the comment. Uncle Nathan was wealthy but he had never had an idea in his head. His idea of success had been to buy fabric cheap and have it cut and sewn into garments which he still sold cheap, but not so cheap that he didn't make a profit. His success was predicated upon longevity: he had made small amounts of money for enough years to turn them into large amounts of money. Solly was going to make large amounts of money, but not by outlasting the American dollar. He was going to make it with the brilliant sparkle of his ideas that no one else had.

So far, the big idea had just eluded him. The Mark Spitz gold medal memorial key chains hadn't made it. Battlestar Galactica boardgames had bombed. No one had wanted his pirated eight-track tape of the background music from King Kong II.

He had printed up 20,000 Elvis Presley T-shirts, couldn't sell them, and had unloaded them for a dime on the dollar. Two weeks later, Elvis Presley had died, the T-shirts were worth their weight in gold, but they then belonged to someone else.

In desperation, he had developed a racetrack betting system based on the biorhythms of horses, but when he found out that it only lost money, he stopped playing it and tried to sell it by direct mail to gamblers. No one bought it.

When the balance in his bank account was down

to $20,000, from the half-million he had been left by his father, Solly Martin decided it was time to rethink his career as a businessman.

He decided he had lost the common touch. He was so brilliant, so far ahead of his time, so advanced beyond the rabble, that he had forgotten to stay in touch with what they thought and believed. He would move immediately to reestablish his contact with the buying public.

He told his mother, "I'm going to open a store."

His Uncle Nathan looked up from his plate. "He's going to sell sand to Arabs," he told Solly's mother. "Open a branch in Iran. Sell Stars of David. A businessman yet."

He attacked the last helpless kreplach which skidded around the plate away from his fork.

"Yeah," Solly said. "Well, maybe that's not such a bad idea. Think of all the Stars of David you could sell to people who want to burn them in demonstrations and things. Want to deface them. You ever think of that?"

"No, thank God," his uncle said. "If I thought of things like that, I would be sleeping in the street, making soup in an empty tomato can, Mister Businessman. Hah!" He looked at Solly and showed his yellowed teeth.

Solly Martin left the house. He felt uncomfortable. His uncle was too old-country to know anything about today and the movements that were going on in the world of marketing. And besides he had gotten uncomfortably close.

Solly had just bought a building off Main Street in White Plains, New York, in the heart of fashionable Westchester County. He was going to sell Middle Eastern imports, which could now be bought for a song with so much of the Middle East going under economically.

Buy cheap and sell dear. Was anything simpler?

Unfortunately, Middle Eastern countries obviously did not regard shipping schedules as the life-and-death matter that American companies did, so on the day Solly's store was to open, all that had arrived were two boxes of Islamic crescent pins, one box in cheap gold metal and the other in mother of pearl, and seventeen cartons of banners bearing the Palestine Liberation Organization symbol, which Solly did not remember ordering.

He complained on the telephone to his supplier who, when he had taken Solly's order, had wanted to be called Phil, but now explained that his name was really Faud Banidegh, and said that he had ordered all Solly's supplies, he had, but it was America's fault, trying to make Iranian businessmen in America look bad to help restore an imperialist regime in Iran, but what could one expect of imperialists who slept with Zionists, and it was too late for Solly to stop payment on his check because it had already been cashed.

Solly's first customer came in, looked around the store and left without saying a word.

His second customer was a woman with a gray pants suit, and graying reddish-dyed hair. She looked around, then stood at the counter, fingering an Islamic crescent.

Solly appeared before her. "Can I help you?" he said.

"Yes," she said. "Hold still." Then she spat in his face, dropped the crescent on the floor and ground it under her heel before leaving.

They were the last two people to enter the Little

5

Flower of the East Shoppe in White Plains, except for bill collectors, meter readers, and delivery men sent by the lunatic Iranian, Faud Banidegh, who seemed intent on burying Solly Martin under mountains of Islamic crescents, half in cheap golden metal and the other half in mother of pearl.

Solly decided to advertise, but when the local newspaper said it wanted cash in advance, Solly put signs up on his windows. BIG SALE drew no one. CLOSEOUT did no better. Neither did ABSOLUTELY LAST CLOSEOUT. FINAL DAYS brought him no customers, but three people did stop in front of his store and applaud and at night, one wrote under the sign "About time."

WE'RE GIVING IT AWAY brought in one teenager under the assumption that the Little Flower of the East Shoppe was a porn parlor, but when he saw no peep movies, he snarled in disgust and walked out.

On the day his money ran out, and still the boxes arrived bearing Islamic crescents and PLO banners, Solly decided to do what he guessed most American businessmen did when faced with a disaster. He went to a saloon, and there he found out what many American businessmen did when really faced with a disaster, and it wasn't drink.

Solly told his tale of woe to two men sitting next to him at the bar.

They cracked their knuckles a lot and looked at each other and nodded as they listened.

"Now I'm not only broke, but I owe that Arab my lungs," Solly said.

"You miscalculated the American psyche," said the shorter man, whose name was Moe Moscalevitch.

6

The taller of the two had the face of a beagle that had been cast in wax and hung on a sunny wall to melt. He nodded. "Definitely correct," he said. "A miscalculation of the American psycho."

"Psyche," corrected Moe Moscalevitch. Ernie Flammio looked chastened. He said to Solly, "There's only one way out." Solly looked up quickly.

"I'm too young to die," Solly said.

"Who said die?" asked Flammio.

"Correctitude," said Moscalevitch, who said things like that a lot. "Nobody mentioned your impending demise."

"That's right," said Ernie Flammio. "No one mentioned your attending derise."

"Impending demise," said Moe Moscalevitch.

"Right. Impending demise," said Flammio.

"What then?" asked Solly Martin.

The two men did not answer him immediately. They called over the bartender, who filled their glasses. They paid for the drink, the first they had bought since bumping into the self-pitying Martin, then took him to a corner of the room, where they sat at a table and talked in whispers.

"We're talking about a fire," said Moscalevitch.

"A fi—" Martin started to speak, but Flammio clapped a big bony hand over his mouth.

"That's right," Moscalevitch whispered. "A fire. Just a match. Snap, crackle, flash, your problems are solved. You collect from the insurance company. You get your money back. You can start over again somewhere else with some other wonderful idea."

Solly was calculating. A fire wasn't bad. He remembered his family always joked about Uncle

Nathan's annual fire, which usually seemed to break out when business turned seasonally bad. A fire had something else going for it, too. It beat suicide, which was the only thing Solly Martin had been able to think of on his own.

"Well," Solly said and took a big drink from his vodka screwdriver. He looked around suspiciously to made sure no one was eavesdropping. The two men nodded approval. "A fire," Solly said. "But how . . ."

"The how is up to us," said Ernie Flammio. "We ain't called the Fire Twins for nothing."

Solly could have kissed him. How nice of these two men to help him out this way. It was three drinks later that he realized the help was not just altruistic. It was a $2,000 act of assistance, payable in advance.

He could get that much from his mother without a problem. And then he would find a new business. One that the public would be smart enough to patronize. He was tired of having the public's stupidity make him into a failure. The next time, he would give them what they wanted. They wanted stupid, he'd give them stupid. Boy, would he give them stupid. They wanted hamburgers made out of sawdust, they'd get them. They want chicken with coating made of 712 toxic chemicals, they got it. Fish that no one who had ever smelled an ocean could eat? No problem. He was finished with trying to improve America's life. He was going to give them all what they deserved.

When he woke the next morning, Solly Martin had a terrible headache. It got worse when he remembered what had happened the night before.

He wondered if Moe Moscalevitch and Ernie

Flammio would be waiting for him at the Little Flower of the East Shoppe, but they weren't. Instead, they called him shortly after 11 A.M.

"It won't do for us to be seen there," Moscalevitch said.

"No. Right," said Solly. He wondered how he could call this whole thing off.

"It'll be tomorrow night, kid," Moscalevitch said. "Just remember, leave the back door unlocked when you go. We'll bust it up so it looked like burglars. And you make sure you're out of town somewhere, so no one can pin anything on you."

"All right," said Solly. He held onto the telephone a moment, building up his courage to tell them to call it off. Then his eyes lighted on the stack of bills sent him by the Iranian, Faud Banidegh, and he gulped and said, "Yeah. Tomorrow night. All right."

Served them right. Served them all right. Maybe those two could set a fire that would spread all the way to Iran. Maybe he could take his insurance winnings and get Moe and Ernie to burn down Banidegh's office in New York. Maybe . . . maybe . . . and a glimmer of an idea entered Solly Martin's mind.

He knew he shouldn't be there. He knew it was risky. But Solly Martin couldn't stay away from his store the next night. The idea that had been throbbing gently in his brain was beginning to take shape, and he wanted to watch, to learn, to see if something could really be made to work.

To protect himself, he had gone to his mother's for dinner. When she wasn't looking, he had set the kitchen clock three hours ahead, then slipped a

9

sleeping pill into her glass of Manischewitz grape wine. As he started to nod off at the table, he called her attention to the clock, which read midnight, and told her, "It's midnight, Momma, I think I'll go to bed here, too."

He had put the old woman to sleep, then hustled downstairs into his car and driven up to White Plains. Now he sat, parked in a darkened side street, diagonally across from the front entrance to his store. The Little Flower of the East Shoppe looked even more dismal and forlorn at night that it did in the daytime. No emptier, but sadder somehow.

He waited, hunched down in the car, for almost an hour before he saw someone walking toward the store on the deserted shopping center street.

He had expected Moe Moscalevitch and Ernie Flammio. He had not expected a scrawny young boy with pipecleaner arms sticking out of his raggy T-shirt and pants that were two years and three inches too short.

The boy paused under a street lamp. In the amber-bright light, Martin could see he was about thirteen years old. He had a mop of flaming red hair and a face that looked as if it belonged on a poster urging people to send the underprivileged to summer camp.

The boy looked around, then darted into the alley between Martin's store and the next building. Solly leaned back in his car seat. His brow wrinkled. Who was the kid? The two arsonists had said nothing about a kid helping them.

Only a few minutes later, Moscalevitch and Flammio walked rapidly down the street. Flammic carried a bag. Without hesitating or looking around,

10

they turned sharply into the alley next to the store and headed for the back. Solly Martin nodded his head. He was satisfied now that the kid had been a lookout.

The back door to Solly Martin's shop wasn't just unlocked; it was wide open, and Moe Moscalevitch grunted his annoyance. The kid Martin was a putz. No one noticed an unlocked door, but an open door was an invitation for neighbors to call the police.

He was about to say something to Ernie Flammio, when he heard a sound inside the store and stopped in mid-stride. He wheeled toward his taller companion and raised a finger to his mouth, cautioning silence. Flammio nodded. The two men listened.

Lester McGurl hummed under his breath as he tossed papers from behind Solly Martin's counter onto the floor. He loved it. He just loved it.

He pulled PLO banners off the shelves, opened them and tossed them into one of the corners. When he had first started in the store, he had glanced every few seconds at the front windows to make sure that he wasn't seen, but that caution was forgotten now. He loved what he was doing, and sometimes he wished that people would stop by to watch. He threw more papers onto the floor.

Outside, Ernie Flammio hissed to Moe Moscalevitch, "He's humming 'I don't want to set the world on fire.'"

"No, he's not," said Moscalevitch. "The name of that ditty is 'My Old Flame.'"

"Oh. Something like that," Flammio said. "What's he doing now?"

11

"I don't know." Moscalevitch was crouched down behind the open door. He peeked into the store. "He's just a kid."

"Maybe that Martin hired him, too."

"No," said Moscalevitch. "Just a free-lancer, I think."

He stood up and walked through the door. Ernie Flammio, carrying the bag containing gasoline and lengths of twine that had been soaked in potassium nitrate and allowed to dry to be used as fuses, followed him.

"What are you doing in here?" Moscalevitch said to the back of young Lester McGurl.

The skinny boy wheeled and looked at the two men. Instinctively, he backed away. In the faint glimmer from the street lights, filling the store with a dull orange glow, he could see their faces. They were adults, and he did not like adults. Not these, not any. He had never seen the men before, but he had seen that kind of face before. He had seen them at orphanages and foster homes, and the faces came connected to heavy, strong hands that had spent years beating on Lester McGurl. Until recently. Until he had found a way to stop the beatings.

Even from across the room, he could smell the gasoline they were carrying and he knew, without thinking, what they were here for.

"This is *my* fire," he said petulantly, still backing away. "Why don't you just go and leave me alone?"

Solly Martin knew it was wrong, but he had gotten tired of waiting. And besides, he wanted to know more about this whole arson thing.

He got out of his car and walked through the alley separating his store from the next building. The rear door to his store was open, and he paused, shaking his head. He didn't know anything about arson-for-hire, but it seemed dumb to leave the door open so anyone might notice and call the police. He walked toward the door, then heard voices inside. They were talking too loudly for his liking.

He didn't think that was cool. He considered getting the hell out of there, before those two incompetent loonies got him arrested as well as themselves. Screw it, he decided. It was his money. He would just walk in and tell them to knock off the noise.

He paused in the doorway and saw Moscalevitch and Flammio standing only a few feet from him, their backs to him. At the other corner of the store was the young kid.

Before Solly could say anything, Moscalevitch spoke.

"What do you mean, *your* fire? This is a bought and paid-for job."

He and Flammio took a step forward.

"I don't want to hurt you," Solly Martin heard the boy say. It was a child's voice, too small and too thin to carry the threat that was in the words.

Flammio laughed.

"That's a gas," he said. "*You* hurt *us*? What are we gonna do with this creep, Moe?"

"I think we're gonna have to leave him here," Moscalevitch said.

Martin watched as the two men walked slowly toward the youth. The boy said again, "I'm warning you."

Flammio laughed again.

13

The boy spread his arms far out to his sides, as if he were planning to fly away.

If he hadn't seen it with his own eyes, Solly Martin would never have believed it.

The young boy put his arms out to his side, just as Flammio and Moscalevitch charged toward him.

Then the boy started to shine. Right before Martin's eyes, he started to shine, first giving off a faint blue glimmer as if a gas flame were surrounding his body. The glow grew in intensity, enveloping the thin young body like a spiritual aura. Moscalevitch and Flammio stopped charging. They stood rooted in the middle of the store, and then the boy pointed his arms and fingertips forward at the two men, and the blue aura surrounding him began to change in color. First, it turned violet, and then as the blue vanished, more redness appeared—more and more, brighter and brighter. Then there was an orange glow around the boy, the throbbing color of a poker heated in a coal fire, and it pained Solly's eyes to stare at it. But he continued to stare, and through the orange haze, he could see the boy's face, and the boy's eyes were narrowed and glinting, and his mouth was wide open and his teeth shone in a broad smile of pure joy.

Then, as if the two men were the negative poles of a battery and the boy a giant positive generator, flashes of orange light darted across the room and enveloped the men's bodies. Solly Martin stifled a scream. The men's clothes were burned off their bodies instantly, and the orange flame was consuming them, and before Martin's eyes, they seemed to be melting, sinking slowly toward the floor.

14

They never screamed, and Martin knew they were dead, and then the can of gasoline Flammio had been carrying exploded and splashed flame all over the store, and instantly papers and PLO banners began to burn.

At the back of the store, young Lester McGurl was still glowing. He spun around and pointed his hands toward the far wall, and flashes of flame jumped forward from his fingers. Where the long sparks of flames hit the wall, the dried old wood began to burn immediately.

The boy looked around. He nodded. The two arsonists' bodies in the middle of the floor were still burning, fat sputtering from their carcasses, and where the splashes touched the wood of the floor, the floor began to burn. The rest of the store was burning, too, and the young boy began to change color slowly, backing from orange to red to purple to blue, and then back to his normal color, almost as if he were a battery and the last drop of juice had been drained from him.

Lester McGurl ran toward the rear door. Solly Martin made one of those judgments that, later, he would ask himself where he got the courage to make.

As the youth ran by him, Solly grabbed him around his skinny shoulders and before the startled boy could fight, Solly hissed, "We've got to get out of here. Come on. I'm your friend. I'm not going to hurt you."

He was surprised at the frailty of the boy's bones. It felt as if he had a bird in his hands. The boy offered him no resistance, almost as if he had no energy left. Solly Martin led him quickly down the alley toward his waiting car.

He wanted to get out of there before the police arrived. He knew that, in the crook of his arm, he had the commercial commodity he had always been looking for.

He had never in his life been able to make a dollar selling anything to the general public, but he was going to have a different clientele now. He was going to be selling fires to people who wanted fires, and in Lester McGurl he had the commodity that separated him from anyone else peddling arson in the United States.

Lester McGurl let himself be put into the front seat of the car.

When Solly got in behind the wheel, he saw that Lester was staring at him.

"You going to hit me?" McGurl said.

"No," said Solly. "I'm going to feed you."

The boy shook his head. "You're going to beat me," he insisted.

"No, I'm not," said Solly. "I'm going to make you rich. And I'm going to give you all the fires you want. How's that sound?"

"I'll believe it when I see it," Lester McGurl said.

"Believe it," said Solly Martin.

They were gone before the fire engines arrived.

CHAPTER TWO

His name was Remo, and the sand that landed on his belly was damp and cold.

He opened one eye to look at the three-year-old blonde girl who squatted over a long ditch she was digging in the sand of the beach.

"Why are you throwing sand on my belly?" Remo asked her. He was in a bathing suit, lying on his back on a Mickey Mouse towel in the bright summer heat of Point Pleasant Beach at the New Jersey shore.

"I'm digging a moke," the girl said without looking up. Her little tin shovel—the first Remo had seen in years because he thought only plastic shovels were being made—flashed down into the sand without pause, digging up a small spoon-sized scoop and throwing it past her left shoulder, where most of it landed on Remo's stomach again. Her lips were pressed together tightly as she concentrated on her dazzling feat of earth-moving.

"What's a moke?" Remo asked.

"It's what you dig around a cassoo," the little girl said. "My big sister Ardaff told me all about it."

"That's not a moke," Remo said. "It's a moat." He wiped the sand from his stomach. "And besides,

18

where's your castle? Why are you building a moat around a castle when you don't have a castle? I think it's just a trick to throw more sand on my belly."

The girl kept digging. More sand kept landing on Remo's stomach. Some of it, dryer than the rest, landed in his face. "I'm making the moke first 'cause it's easier to make the moke," she said.

"Moat," Remo said.

"Moke," the girl agreed. "Then I'll make the cassoo." She had long blonde pigtails, dotted with fresh wet sand that glistened like diamond chips. Her body was pink, not yet burned by the sun, and it seemed made of ovals—curvy, round, and soft with no discernible muscles.

"Why'd you decide to build it next to me when you've got this whole beach to build it on?" Remo asked. He spread his arms wide to indicate the expanse of beach and got a shovel full of sand in his unprotected face for his trouble. He turned over on his side and propped himself up on one arm to look at the girl.

"'Cause I thought if dragons comes, you gonna defend my cassoo," the girl said. For the first time, she looked at him and smiled. Her eyes were sky blue, and her little baby teeth were even and sparkled white like pearls.

"Why me?" Remo said. "You ever see a dragon?"

"'Cause you looks nice," the girl said. "And my big sister Ardaff told me all about dragons, and they're bigger than me."

"You think I look nice?" Remo said. He looked down at his hands. They had been responsible for hundreds of deaths, and while the bloodstains weren't visible, they were there—in his mind. Remo

19

wondered when anyone had last thought he was nice.

"Sure, you're nice," she said with the un-self-consciousness of the very young. "Very nice." She was back to digging, tossing sand over her shoulder at Remo.

"I'm not nice."

"Yes, you are."

"Will you marry me?"

"Not until I build my cassoo," she said.

"I guess I'll just have to help you build it, won't I?" Remo said.

The girl had dug a ditch in a roughly square pattern, four feet on a side. Remo knelt alongside her, and the hands that had been trained to kill became as gentle as a surgeon's but more precise than any surgeon's ever had been.

Using the girl's water bucket, Remo wet sand and scooped it up into large rectangular shapes. Using fingertips as punches, he knocked out window holes in the sides of the large walls. Then, atop the base, he built twisting towers and battlements, piling sand on top of sand as the girl sipped her breath, knowing the towers must fall. But Remo could feel through his fingertips the internal tension of the sand, and just at the moment when he knew it would collapse of its own weight, he backed off and began working on another turret.

The castle was a creation from Oz, mock stone towers reaching into the sky, standing taller than the little girl herself. People on the beach began to watch the structure, now almost six feet tall, something from a fairy tale.

Remo stepped back away from the castle, ringed

by its dismal meandering excuse of a moat and said, "There we go. Marry me now?"

"After I play a little bit. You're really nice." She grabbed his hand and pulled him down to her so she could kiss his cheek. As Remo stood up, he saw all the people on the beach watching them, and he felt self-conscious and embarrassed.

"Always the way," he said. "Always my luck to fall in love with a woman who wants to play a little bit first."

Behind the crowd, he saw the person he had been waiting for—a tall, spare man with thinning gray hair, wearing a gray three-piece suit even in the summer heat of the Jersey shore. He was standing on the narrow boardwalk, looking down toward Remo, and when their eyes met, he nodded. Remo nodded back.

"I'll be back in a little while," he told the girl. He squeezed her hand and then walked across the hot sand to where Dr. Harold W. Smith, head of the super-secret agency CURE, waited on a bench for him. Remo walked slowly, oblivious to the scorching heat underfoot.

Remo sat next to Smith, brushing dried sand from his chest and stomach. Remo was tall and lean, and his body was that of an athlete, trim and trained but not exceptional. The only thing that might have called attention to him were his thick wrists, which he kept working by rotating his fists, as if his wrists were sore. He had dark hair, as dark as his midnight pools of his eyes, which were buried deep behind high cheekbones that sometimes made him seem almost Oriental.

"I'm glad to see you're maintaining your usual low profile," Smith said.

21

"You think the kid's an enemy agent?" Remo said. "Wait here, I'll go kill her." He started to rise.

Smith sighed. "Sit down," he said. "Why does every conversation start off the same way?"

"Because you're always dumping on me right at the start because I'm not hiding behind a bush or something," Remo said. "Hey, this is the Jersey shore. Half those guys on the beach are Jersey politicians. They're watching the ocean trying to figure out a way to steal it. The other half are federal agents, watching the politicians. Nobody's watching me."

He looked at Smith, then back at the little blonde girl in the red bathing suit. She was squatting next to her sand castle. Her lips were moving, busily engaged in play conversation with herself. Remo smiled. It was nice to do something nice for someone. Maybe he was nice after all.

"What's on your mind?" he asked Smith.

"It's Ruby," Smith said.

Ruby was Ruby Jackson Gonzales, the light-skinned black woman who was Smith's assistant. Except for Smith, Remo, and whoever was president of the United States at the time, she was the only person who knew of the existence of the secret agency CURE, which had been set up years before to fight crime without paying too much attention to the niceties of the law. Remo was its killer arm. Remo thought of Ruby, then remembered her screeching rock-splitting voice and told Smith, "I don't want to hear about it. She's your problem. You hired her. What's she trying to do, overthrow you and sell stock in the organization?"

"She wants to quit," Smith said softly. He folded his hands across the attaché case on his lap. Remo realized he could not remember ever seeing Smith without an attaché case, and he wondered what was in it that Smith kept so close to him all the time. It was as if the CURE director wore a four-piece suit: trousers, vest, jacket, and attaché case.

"Good," Remo said. "Let her quit. I'm tired of listening to her yell at me all the time anyway."

"It's not that easy," Smith said. And of course it wasn't. Remo knew that. Someone out there who knew about CURE but did not work for it was too big a problem and too big a threat to endure.

"Why does she want to quit?" Remo asked.

"She says she's bored. The work is dull. She wants to go back to her wig business and make some real money."

"Try giving her a raise?" Remo asked.

"I tried that."

"What'd she say?"

"She said there wasn't enough money in the world to make the job less boring."

"That doesn't sound like Ruby," Remo said. "That woman likes money. She must really be bored." He watched the little girl moving her tiny arm in and out of the windows of the sand castle, playing some fantasy adventure scripted in her mind. "You want me to talk to her?" Remo asked.

"No," Smith said.

"What then?" Remo asked.

"I want you to . . . to remove her."

Remo wheeled about and looked at Smith's face. It was as impassive as ever, staring out at the gray sea.

"Ruby?" Remo said. "You want me to kill her?" He studied Smith's face, but it was unchanged,

23

chartless, as smooth as the waveless ocean. But he nodded curtly.

"That's right," Remo said bitterly. "You just sit there and nod, but what we're talking about is killing somebody. One of our own. Did you forget? Ruby saved me and Chiun once. And you sit there like some kind of gray mummy and shake your head up and down and to you, that's shaking your head, but to me that means go kill somebody, go kill a friend."

"Remo, I know how you feel. But she knew the risks when she signed on. I don't know why you think I like this."

"Because you do like it, you bloodless . . ."

Remo stopped. He had been looking toward the water, and he saw it coming. A big tanned blond man with shoulder-length hair, carrying a surfboard under his arm, was running along the beach, and maliciously, he plowed through the sand castle that Remo had built. Even a hundred feet away, Remo could hear his happy exultant laugh. The little girl in the red bathing suit looked at the running man in surprise and shock, then looked at the wreckage of her dream castle, then sank slowly into a squat, crying. Even from his distance, Remo could see her back racking with sobs.

"Excuse me," Remo told Smith. "Wait here." He jumped lightly over the boardwalk railing, down onto the hot sand, and ran over to the little girl and the wreckage of the castle.

Tears streamed down her cheeks. She looked at Remo with hurt in her face.

"You were 'upposed to watch out for dragons," she said. "And now look what happened."

"Don't get on my case," Remo said. "We're not married yet. Anyway, we'll fix it up again."

"We will?"

"You betcha," Remo said. He sent the girl to fill her pail with water, and with skilled hands, he quickly rebuilt the castle, even taller and grander than before. As he worked, the girl rocked from foot to foot, watching him, barely able to contain her happiness.

When he was done, she looked at him with love, and he brushed the tears from her eyes. She said, "You know I'm not allowed to get married. My big sister Ardaff said I'm too little."

"I know," Remo said.

"But when I'm bigger, I'll marry you."

"I hope so," Remo said.

"Because you're nice," the girl said.

"Thank you," Remo said. He stood up. "Now, you play here and have a nice time, because I have to go."

"Do you want to go?"

"No," said Remo. "But I've got something to do."

"Will I see you again?"

"No," Remo said.

"Oh," she said, accepting that with the resignation of children to whom most of life is still a sad surprise. "I love you."

"I love you, too," Remo said.

He walked away from the girl, down toward the next beach where a cove created by two long rock jetties caught the waves and created enough turmoil from the usually placid ocean to allow for minor-league surfboarding.

The big blond surfer stood on a small hillock of

sand overlooking the beach, like a Greek god surveying his domain. His surfboard was stuck in the sand in front of him like a Persian shield.

Remo walked around in front of him. The young man was bigger than Remo and huskier. He looked as if he drank suntan oil for sustenance.

"You're in my sun," he said unpleasantly.

"You knocked down that little girl's sand castle," Remo said.

"She shouldn't build things in the traffic lane," the blond said.

"That's not why you knocked it down," Remo said.

"Oh? Why then?"

"Because you're not a nice person," Remo said. "Now, I am. I have it on the very highest authority that I am a nice person."

"Nice guys finish last."

"Not anymore they don't," Remo said.

He lifted the surfboard out of the sand, raised it a foot above the level of the beach, then slammed the fiberglass panel back down into the sand. To get there, it had to pass through the toes of the young man's right foot. It did.

The man looked down at his foot. He lifted the front of it and saw that his toes were missing.

"My foot, my foot," he yelled. "My toes." He looked at Remo. "What . . . ?"

Remo smiled.

"Hang five," he said casually, as he walked off.

He walked straight back to the boardwalk, where Smith still sat on the bench.

"Smitty," said Remo, "I've got something to tell you, but first I'm going to do you a favor. Does Ruby know you're meeting with me?"

Smith said, "Yes."

"Then she knows what's on your mind," Remo said. "She knows what you came here to tell me. I'd suggest you make sure that she didn't plant a bomb in your car."

"It's all right," Smith said. "I came down on the bus."

"You would," Remo said.

"You said you had something to tell me?" Smith said.

"Yes. You can take this assignment and stuff it. You can take this job and stuff it. I'm done."

"Just like that?" Smith said.

"Just like that," Remo said.

"Mind telling me why?"

"No. I don't mind. I'm too nice to work for you people. That's why."

Remo turned and walked away. At the steps leading to the sidewalk, he paused, then walked back to Smith.

"As long as it doesn't matter anymore," he said, "I'm going to satisfy my curiosity." He slapped aside Smith's hands and opened the gray leather briefcase.

Inside was a portable telephone and a pill bottle. There was one pill inside.

"Mind telling me what this is for?" Remo said.

"Of course not," said Smith. "The phone's hooked up to CURE's computers. If I need to, I can dial a number and erase everything that's on our tapes, all trace of our having existed."

"And the pill?" Remo asked.

"If I have to erase the tapes," Smith said, "I'd have to erase me, too. It's for that." He looked at Remo, his face as bland and unconcerned as ever.

27

The answer gave Remo little satisfaction. He slammed down the lid of the case. "I hope you don't ever have to use it," Remo said.

"Thank you," Smith said.

Remo walked out into the small town. He wandered the streets of small, garage-size houses that for the most part constituted New Jersey shore architecture. The tough part was still to come. How to explain to Chiun, his teacher and trainer, that he had quit CURE. Remo had quit before, many times before, but something always seemed to bring him back. This time, there would be no coming back. He was sure of it and just as sure that this would offend Chiun, the reigning Master of Sinanju, head of an ancient house of Korean assassins who had been assassin to king and shah, emperor and pharaoh, and to whom the only thing more sacred than fulfilling one's contract was the necessity of getting paid on time. Preferably in gold.

Chiun would not understand. He had taken Remo soon after Remo, then a young policeman, had been framed for a murder he didn't commit and sent to an electric chair that didn't work, and Chiun had trained Remo Williams to work for CURE. And in the years of training, he had changed Remo's body and his mind, had made him something more than other men. He had made him a man who used his body and senses fully, but he had never been able to make Remo a Korean. And he would not understand Remo's wanting to leave the service of an employer who always paid on time. To Chiun, Smith was the best of Emperors.

Remo had thought he was wandering aimlessly, but when he looked up, he was back in front of the Norfield Inn, where he and Chiun were staying, and now he walked in the side entrance and up the worn carpeted stairs to their second-floor room.

Chiun was not there. Remo thanked God for small favors and packed his overnight bag with his only belongings—a change of underwear, a tooth-brush, a razor.

He slipped off his bathing suit, showered, and changed into black chinos and a black T-shirt. Maybe he was a nice person after all. He had been raised in an orphanage, but who knew, maybe he came from a long line of nice people. Maybe his ancestors had always been nice.

"Nice guy, Remo Williams," he mumbled to himself. "Proud descendant of an unbroken string of nice guys."

He took his bag and walked down to the small backyard swimming pool behind the ancient hotel and found Chiun sitting in a corner of the yard, underneath a tree, his hands folded quietly in his lap. Light breezes blew the wisps of white hair alongside Chiun's lined parchment face. The ancient Korean was staring ahead at the water of the pool, which was rippling slightly from the agitation of the filtering system.

Remo stood in front of him silently until Chiun looked up.

"Chiun, I've quit."

"Again?"

"For good this time."

"Why?" Chiun asked.

"Because I think I'm a nice person. Do you think I'm a nice person?"

"I think you are an idiot. Sit here and talk to me." Remo sat on the grass next to Chiun.

"Smitty wanted me to kill Ruby," Remo said.

"Oh," said Chiun. Remo could tell by the tone of voice that Chiun was concerned at this.

"Because she wants to leave CURE," Remo explained.

"And now that you have betrayed your employer, you think she will live? You think that Emperor Smith will just say, oh, Remo will not remove Ruby and therefore Ruby must live? You know he will not say that, Remo. He will take steps to dispatch Ruby another way. So what have you gained? Instead of doing what you have been trained to do and guaranteeing that her death will be painless and swift, you have made it likely that she will suffer at the hands of some idiot. But she will still be dead. You will have accomplished nothing."

"Chiun, I know all that. But I just don't want to be part of an organization that kills their best—like Ruby. I just can't handle that anymore. Let me ask you—would you kill Ruby?"

"If my emperor said to ply the assassin's art upon her, then I would. The decision to do that is emperor's business and therefore not mine. I am not an emperor. I am an assassin."

"Just like that, you'd kill her?"

"Just like that, I would do as my emperor wished."

"Smitty may send you after me," Remo said. "Will you take that assignment?"

"I love you as a son, because you are my son," Chiun said, watching the shiny water of the pool.

"I know," Remo said. "And you love your thousands of years of Sinanju tradition."

"Yes, I do. As you should."

"I'm leaving," Remo said.

"Where will you go?"

"I don't know. I want to think about myself and just who I am. I'll let you know where I'll be if you need to find me."

Chiun nodded.

"Will you be all right here?" Remo asked.

"Yes. I will be all right."

Remo stood up. He looked down awkwardly at Chiun, wondering what he might say to break the silence, to lift the tension of the moment.

"Well, so long," he said.

Chiun nodded.

When Remo walked through the gate, Chiun stared after him for a long time. Then softly to himself, he said, "Foolish child. No one will kill Ruby Gonzales all that easily."

CHAPTER THREE

After driving Dr. Harold W. Smith to the bus station, Ruby Jackson Gonzales had not gone back to Folcroft Sanitarium, the building in Rye, New York, which served as the cover for CURE's operations and housed the massive computer network of the crime-fighting agency.

For the past four days, she had cautiously been cleaning out her desk—carrying personal belongings home at night in her purse—and now she went directly to the three-room luxury apartment she rented in Rye, to pick up her suitcases, packed the night before.

She and Smith had not discussed where he was going, but she knew from the charge bills that had come across her desk that Remo and Chiun were at the Jersey shore. And she knew, too that Smith had made the appointment with Remo himself, a task which normally would have been Ruby's. That meant Smith didn't want Ruby to know what they were talking about.

Fat chance. She knew the only way anybody left CURE would be in a box, and Smith was on his way to tell Remo to ice Ruby. Let him try; before the ice arrived, this coldcut was going to be long gone.

A half-hour after Smith's bus had left town, Ruby was aiming her white Continental south also, toward Newark, New Jersey, a city where she had relatives and where her black face would be just one among hundreds of thousands of black faces. There she would figure out what to do next. Going home to Norfolk, Virginia, at the moment was out of the question; it would be the first place they'd look for her.

As she was driving out of Rye on the Cross-Westchester expressway, an idea came to her, and instead of taking the Tappan Zee bridge to New Jersey, she turned south on the New York Thruway and headed into New York City. There was something she wanted to do first.

CHAPTER FOUR

Newark, New Jersey. Crossroad of 300,000 private lives. Gigantic stage on which are played a thousand dramas daily.

And on this day, three special dramas.

Remo was never supposed to go back to the town because he had left it dead. But he had been there once since, and St. Theresa's orphanage had been an old soot-covered brick building, with the windows and doors boarded up, a dead building waiting for the rest of the neighborhood to catch up with it.

That had been a couple of years earlier, and now the neighborhood had caught up with the old orphanage. The street was a collection of empty lots and fire-gutted buildings. Even in the daytime, rats scurried across the street. Remo parked his car there and looked up at the old orphanage building. It was dead still, just as much of Newark was dead, just as Remo Williams—that old Remo Williams who had grown up in this building and been punished with rulers across the knuckles when he'd been bad—just as he was dead too. He sighed. What had he expected? A brass band and a memorial plaque designating this as the spot where Remo Williams was raised? There were no brass plaques erected in this kind of neighborhood. Junkies stole brass.

The idea of tracing his parentage, finding out just when and how and why he had gotten to St. Theresa's as a boy, suddenly seemed like an insurmountable problem to him. He put the car in gear and drove off. He would think about it tomorrow. First, he would get a hotel room.

Lester McGurl, who had decided he liked to be called "Sparky," already had a hotel room.

He was sitting in it now, the television tuned in to an afternoon soap opera, a drinking glass from the bathroom on the floor five feet in front of the chair in which he lounged.

The boy had filled out. In a few weeks since had had met Solly Martin, he had gained almost twenty pounds, and now all that poundage was encased in an expensive suit that fit correctly. Still, Sparky would have loved the suit even if it hadn't fit, simply because it was his suit, owned by him, not a hand-me-down that had been rubbed raw by a half-dozen wearers before it finally got to him.

He pulled a match from a book, scratched it lit, and tossed it toward the glass on the floor. It hit the edge of the glass, then dropped back onto the floor, where it burned a moment, charring a black spot in the nylon rug before sputtering out. The glass was half filled with burned matches; the floor pocked with a few dozen burned black spots. He ripped out another match and tried again. It dropped into the glass, kept flaming, then set afire the twisted stack of matches inside the container.

Sparky got up from his seat and poured some

water into the glass to extinguish the fire. Solly didn't like it when he broke glasses on the rugs or set fires in hotels. That was the only thing wrong with Solly: he didn't want Sparky to set any fires unless they were paid first for them. But he didn't hit the boy, and he kept him fed and clothed, and he didn't think Sparky was some kind of freak because he had a power to ignite fires, and all in all, Solly Martin was the first kind human being Sparky had ever met. Thinking "father" was painful to Sparky; he had never known a father, just a succession of heavy drinkers and their desperate wives who had used the boy as a vehicle to get foster parents' checks from the state and then had abused and degraded the child. No, not a father. Sparky didn't want to think father. But a big brother. That's what Solly Martin was like to him, and the boy was young enough that he was not embarrassed to say to himself that he loved Solly. He lit another match and flipped it into the glass. Just to make Solly happy, he would not set fire to this hotel when they left.

Two miles away, Ruby pulled her Continental in close to the curb, and three loiterers came down off the front stoop to examine the car more closely.

Ruby opened the car door and made a large show out of setting the anti-theft alarm on the dashboard, then got out of the car and carefully locked the door.

"The Jacksons live here?" she asked one of the three young men, the biggest one with a gigantic bush of an Afro.

"A lot of Jacksons around here," he said sullenly. "Nice car."

38

"That's not a nice car," said one of the other younger men. "A deuce and a quarter, that be a nice car. A hog be a nice car. This just be a Continental."

"Shut up," said the biggest youth. "This car's nice."

"That's right," Ruby said agreeably. "It's a nice car, and I'm the nice owner, and I'm asking you nice one more time. The Jacksons live here?"

The big youth met her eyes, and there was something cool and confident in her look that made him give civility higher marks than usual.

"Fourth floor, back," he said. "Who you?"

"Friend of the family," Ruby said. "Keep an eye on the car, will you? Tell anybody who tries to steal it that there's a poison gas canister inside that goes off if anybody tries to start it without a key."

"Is there?"

"Sure," Ruby said. "But it's not as bad as it sounds. It doesn't really kill them. Just makes them permanently blind."

"That's heavy," the youth said.

Ruby nodded. "Makes it tough to sink jump shots."

She walked quickly up the steps of the old building, whose stone entranceway looked like an entry blank in the international four-letter-word contest. At the top of the stairs, she pushed the Jacksons' bell. Behind her, she heard the three youths discussing vigorously where they might be able to steal a gas mask so they could steal the car without being blinded. She smiled to herself. There was no answer to the doorbell, so she pushed open the unlocked inside door and walked upstairs.

39

There was another bell outside the Jacksons' fourth floor apartment, and it did not work either. She pounded on the door until a voice from inside said, "Stop that banging, for heaven's sakes. Who is it?"

But the door did not open.

"Aunt Lettie, it's Ruby."

"Who?"

"Ruby, your niece."

The door still didn't open. The woman's voice instead asked, "What's your mama's name?"

"Cornelia. And she still smokes her corncob pipe and still wears that silver dollar medal you gave her once."

The door swung open. A little black woman, her face prunelike with age, looked Ruby up and down, then grabbed her by the elbow and pulled her inside.

"Ruby, child, what's the matter? Who's after you?" She quickly closed the door.

"Why do you think somebody's after me, Aunt Lettie?"

" 'Cause not many people comes to Newark just to visit. You all right, girl?"

"I'm fine, Aunt Lettie. Really fine." And when the old woman was finally convinced, she swallowed Ruby up in a hug strong enough to make up for the last ten years in which they hadn't seen each other.

"Come on in, girl. My, my, how pretty and big you got. Come in and talk to your Aunt Lettie. How's your mama? What brings you here, anyway?"

"I thought maybe you could put me up for a few days," Ruby said, as she followed the woman

40

through the neat but sparsely furnished railroad rooms into the kitchen.

"Now I know somebody's after you," Lettie Jackson said, "you wanting to stay here."

Ruby laughed. "Really, Aunt Lettie, you are the most suspicious woman I ever saw. Can't I just want to visit?"

Finally, cajolery and Ruby's obvious good humor pacified the old woman. As Ruby sat at the kitchen table and they talked, the old woman fussed about the kitchen, baking cookies, making tea, insisting that Ruby tell her everything about what she had been doing and how she was and how her mother was and her brother, no-account-Lucius, which the old woman pronounced all in one, as if it were a title and name like Prince Charles or King Edward. No-account-Lucius.

Throughout the day, children drifted into the apartment. Lettie's children, her children's children, her nieces, her nephews. She introduced them all formally to Ruby, daughter of her sister, Cornelia, and Ruby instantly forgot all their names. In the big commune, no one seemed to mind. As it grew dark, Mrs. Jackson explained to Ruby that since she was a guest, she would have a bed to share with only one other person, a sixteen-year-old cousin who had heard that Ruby was in the wig business and wanted her to send two wigs, one for daytime and one for nighttime, so she didn't have to mess with doing her hair.

At last, Ruby went to sleep.

"That's the place?"

Solly Martin looked away from the gray building and at Lester Sparky McGurl.

41

"Yeah," he said. "Then we'll get out of this town and go someplace to make some money." He waved toward the street. "Look at this street," he said, in a voice crisp with indignation. "You'd think anybody with brains'd want to burn down the whole city. But the guy paid us for this building, and so this building's it."

"I better go do it then," Sparky said.

"You all right?" Solly asked. "You all charged up and everything?"

"I guess so. I feel okay," the boy said.

"It knocks me out," Solly said, "how you can just go into a building and wave your arms around and fires start, just like that."

"Me, too," Sparky said. "I never know how it works. It just works. I think it's getting stronger, too. The last time I was really good."

Solly nodded. His eyes looked around the street. It was dark and empty. He was surprised to see a fancy white Continental parked in front of the building. It was not the kind of car one would associate with this street. Sure, there was a myth that welfare chiselers drove Cadillacs and spent all day watching color television, but the fact was that the Cadillacs were usually five years old and burned three quarts of oil going around the block. This Continental didn't look like one of those.

Sparky McGurl slipped out of the car, ran across the deserted street and into the tenement building.

Solly waited. Newark was bad pickings. Everything worth burning down in town had already been burned down. There was only this building, and the goal tonight wasn't property destruction, it was death. The man who had hired them wanted people to die. Solly shrugged. It was all the same to him. He looked at the five-story tenement building. And it was all the same to Sparky. The boy would set anything afire just to see the flames.

Sparky walked quietly up the five flights of stairs. He set his first fire in the top floor left, then sparked off one more on each landing on his way back down. Before the fire was discovered, the stairwells would be burning good, he thought.

Remo walked across the narrow street in front of his hotel, into a park that had been constructed over an underground parking garage.

When he was a child, the nuns of the orphanage would, once a month, take their classes to the Newark museum, but the highlight of the day was stopping later to eat a picnic lunch in this park. It had been elegant then, spotlessly clean, filled with families and students and businessmen.

But it too had succumbed, as had the city itself. As he stepped into the park, Remo felt cheated. Very little of his childhood belonged to him; very little of it had any meaning; but he had remembered this park fondly, and it saddened him to see it now.

Winos sat sprawled on the benches, under the sharp glare of the overhead night lighting. Back in the bushes, Remo could hear young couples giggling in the dark. He walked farther into the park and saw a black drug pusher, wearing almost as much gold around his neck as he had in his mouth, leaning against a small maintenance building.

A pack of youths stood about twenty yards away from the pusher, watching him, and Remo realized they were waiting their turns. First one would come up to the pusher, hand over some money, and

43

get a small package in return. As soon as he started to walk away, another would come up from the waiting group to take his place. Remo wondered if the pusher gave them numbers, as in a bakery, and they had to wait for their number to be called before they could come up to buy their drugs.

Remo looked at three benches before he found one that wasn't broken, then sat down and watched the pusher. He saw the folding money flash white under the overhead light, and he saw the glitter of the little bags the pusher handed out, after first inspecting the money and stuffing it into his pocket.

He wondered where the police were, and he was glad that Sister Mary Margaret had not lived to see this happen in their park. Something began to bubble deep down inside Remo, and at first he thought it was anger, but then he realized it was deeper than anger. It was sorrow. He had thought to get away from the sick world in which he made his living and return to this city and the innocent days of his youth. But the sick world had invaded here, too, and he wondered, just for a fleeting moment, if there were anyplace left in America that was clean, any parks where children still played and didn't have to worry about junkies or winos or pushers.

The pusher saw Remo watching him. He showed no fear, only curiosity, and Remo thought if it had happened years before, when the pusher still had his own teeth and Remo was still a Newark policeman, then the man would have felt fear.

Remo wondered how long he would be able to sustain sorrow before it turned into a compulsion to do something about the cause of that sorrow.

He watched the pusher call the small pack of waiting youths over to him. They were conferring;

44

the pusher was pointing at Remo, and the sorrow went, replaced by a cold, bitter anger. Remo got up from the park bench.

"All right," he said aloud. "Everybody out."

Eight faces turned toward him in surprise.

"You heard me. Everybody out of my park," Remo said. He walked toward the group. They looked at the slim white man, then at each other, exchanging winks and grins.

"Yoah park?" the pusher asked.

"Yeah. My park. Clear out," Remo said.

"This be the people's park," the pusher said. Remo was closer to him now, and the pusher slid back until he was separated from Remo by a wall of young men.

The wall wasn't thick enough. Remo's hand reached in between the youths, grabbed the pusher by the gold chains around his neck and yanked. He flew toward Remo like a ball flying out of a pinball machine chute.

"Hey, don't do that. He be our main man."

"Yeah," grumbled another voice.

But before they could charge Remo, he had the pusher upside down, holding him by his ankles, shaking him. Nickel bags of powder and packages of grass fell from his pockets. Remo shook harder. Money, bills and coins dropped out onto the ground. Every time Remo shook, the pusher's head hit the pavement and he groaned.

"Help me," he moaned. "Free iffen you helps."

"Shut up, you," Remo said. "It's free anyhow." He kicked with his toes at the drugs and money and skittered them across toward the seven young men.

"There. Take what you want. Just get out of my

45

park." He kept shaking the pusher, and more drugs and money fell. Remo kept kicking them toward the group. They seemed to confer with themselves silently, then together, they made a lunge for the drugs and the cash. Within fifteen seconds, the ground was clear again, and the last of their footsteps could be heard vanishing into the night.

"I get them for that," the pusher said.

"It's terrible to realize you're all alone," Remo said, "isn't it?"

"Who are you?" the pusher demanded. "What you want? Stop hitting my head."

Remo turned the pusher right side up. He was as tall as Remo but even thinner.

"Just another student of Sister Mary Margaret," Remo said. "She doesn't like what you're doing to her park."

The pusher was busy straightening his clothing. "I told you, this the people's park." The pusher rubbed his head with his left hand. His right hand reached inside the rear waistband of his trousers and came out with a switchblade knife, which he clicked open and pointed toward Remo. In the overhead light it was brittle and glassy looking.

Remo shook his head. "Too bad," he said. "And I was going to let you go."

"You let shit," the pusher said. "You cost me and I taking it back, sucker. Slice by slice."

He waved the knife at Remo's throat. Remo leaned back. The knife passed harmlessly in front of his face. Then Remo had the pusher, upside down again, dragging him across the pavement toward the park bench. He lifted him up, then dropped him head first into a litter basket. The pusher's head hit with a glassy clunk against the bottles that filled the basket. The pusher didn't fit. Remo pressed down until he did. The cracking of bottles was the only sound after one strong initial groan. Finally, he fit. Only his shoes stuck out of the basket. They were ugly yellow shoes with soles and heels two inches high. Remo bent the man's legs until the shoes fit into the basket, then gave one last push down for good measure. Everything fit now. He wiped his hands over a job well done and went back to sit on the bench.

Ten minutes later, he heard footsteps approaching him. They were loud, heavy footsteps, meant to be loud and heavy. To Remo that spelled cop. Young cop.

Remo looked down at the pavement when the policeman spoke. "What are you doing here, mister?" There was a frightened quaver in his voice.

"Just sitting in my park," Remo said.

"Your park?"

"Yeah. Mine and Sister Mary Margaret's," Remo said.

The patrolman relaxed a little, as if deciding that Remo was a harmless nut case.

"You going to keep sitting there?" he asked Remo after a pause.

"Yes."

"This park is dangerous for a white man," the cop said.

For the first time, Remo looked up from his feet and his eyes met the patrolman's eyes.

"Not tonight," he said. "Not tonight."

Ruby had smelled it before she heard it or saw it. She snapped up into a sitting position in bed.

She took a deep breath. There was no mistaking

47

it; it was a smell that she had lived with since childhood.

Fire.

Ruby jumped out of bed and shook her sixteen-year-old cousin awake.

"Lenora, wake up. The place is on fire."

The teenagers was groggy, slow to respond, and Ruby slapped her hard across the cheek.

The girl woke, shaking her head, her hands going involuntarily to her cheek.

She looked at Ruby, who was already moving toward the door. "The place is on fire," Ruby called over her shoulder. "We've got to wake everybody up."

Working together, the two roused the Jacksons. Almost as if it were a fire drill, the children moved toward the doorway leading to the stairs, each one of the older children taking responsibility for one of the younger children.

Ruby handed eighteen-year-old Molly her suitcase.

"Take this downstairs," she ordered. "Lock it in the trunk of my car and drive my car around the corner, so it doesn't get burned." Without waiting for a reply, she ran along the hallway and began banging on every door she reached.

"Fire," she called. "Everybody awake. It's a fire."

She noticed that the steps leading upstairs were burning, walls and floor ablaze, but she noticed no smell of gasoline or fuel and saw no sign of paper or other tinder that might have been used to start the fire.

She heard footsteps on the steps, and when she looked up, she saw the young man with the huge Afro who had been hanging around outside today.

He was wearing jockey shorts and a T-shirt and was jumping down the steps four at a time.

He started to pass Ruby without slowing, but she reached out her left arm and grabbed him around the waist.

"Where you going?" she said.

"Fire. This place on fire."

"Right," she said. "Do people live upstairs?"

"Sure. Leave me be."

He strained against her left arm and just as he broke loose, Ruby reached into the right pocket of her blue chenille bathrobe and pulled out a small snub-nosed .38 caliber revolver. She put it against his head, between his eyes.

"Upstairs and wake them up."

"Sheeeit."

Ruby shrugged. "Do that or die here. Whatever makes you happy." She cocked the gun.

The young man gulped. "Sheeeit," he repeated. Ruby pressed the gun against his forehead, and he turned and ran up the steps, through the flames, shouting at the top of his voice, "Fire! Fire! Fire!"

Ruby glanced upward and saw flames at the top of the steps. The fire had been set, she realized. It was not one fire, but a string of individual fires set in different places. But who would want to torch this building, except for nutty kids?

No point wondering. She looked around. People were beginning to stream out of the apartments, and she had the fleeting feeling that she was at the circus watching two dozen people get out of one Volkswagen. They marched out of the apartments by handfuls, two and two, four and four, rubbing sleep from their eyes, their tiredness slowing their steps.

Ruby listened for a moment to the continuing bellow of "Fire" on the fifth floor. Then she pushed her way through the stream of kids going downstairs and hopped down to the third floor, where she pounded on more doors and roused more families.

She worked her way down through the building until she was out on the sidewalk. She was glad to see her car had been moved.

Down the street, Ruby could hear the whoops of fire engines. Flames were now licking out through the windows on all five floors of the tenement.

Aunt Lettie ran to her and said, "Oh, girl, I thought you was caught."

"I'm all right," Ruby said. The fire engines were only a block away. "Is everybody out?"

Her aunt looked around at the crowd clustered on the sidewalk. "I think," she said. "Lemme see." She looked again, pointing her finger, ticking off people. "I don't see the Garigles."

Ruby fingered a golden medal around her neck. "Where they live?" she asked.

"Top right, in the front," her aunt said. The fire engines drew nearer. Ruby ran off. Her aunt's voice echoed after her. "Girl, don't go back in there."

The Garigles came out. Ruby didn't. They told Aunt Lettie that they had not seen her niece.

The firemen could not save the building and, ten minutes after they arrived, the roof went, collapsing down into the building like a surrendering soufflé.

The occupants of the house had been pushed back across the street, where they were being interviewed by bored policemen.

When she saw the roof go, Aunt Lettie covered her face with her hands. "Oh, God," she cried. "Oh, my poor Ruby. Oh, child." The Reverend Horatius Q. Witherspool, dressed in an Italian suit of nubby gray silk, put his arm around her in consolation. "It'll be all right, Mrs. Jackson," he said. Even as he spoke, he looked around at the other tenants of the building, as if counting.

An hour later, the walls tumbled in. Firemen working from the middle of the street and the buildings on each side pumped thousands of tons of water into the apartment building. They were not able to enter the ruin for another two hours. They poked around the rubble, but it wasn't until daylight that a rookie fireman found the body. He was rooting around in what had once been the basement. Accompanying him was a photographer from the Newark *Post-Observer*, which had recently been accused of insensitivity to the black community and had therefore posted a standing assignment to get photos of substantial housing fires in the black neighborhoods. It had taken the editorial board two weeks to decide what kind of fires they should take pictures of. Were they insensitive if they ignored fires with fatalities—as if black corpses had no news value? Or were they insensitive if they published fires with fatalities—as if blacks were only newsworthy when dead? The editor-in-chief made the decision: no pictures of fatal fires, unless three or more people were killed at once.

This was a fire without apparent fatalities, so the young photographer was in the basement with the rookie fireman, looking for an interesting picture. The photographer tripped over something that skittered away from him. It was long and about as wide around as a baseball bat. It was dark brown and charred. The photographer bent over to look more closely.

Then he threw up.

It was an arm.

The fireman called for help, and they removed the rubble from over the human remnants.

The photographer told everybody who would listen, "I tripped over his arm. Over there. That's his arm."

"It's not his arm," one fireman said.

"It is. It's his arm. I tripped over it," the photographer said.

"It's not a his. It's an its. Until we identify the body, it ain't a him or a her, it's an its."

When they dug down to the body, there was no way to tell if it had been a man or a woman, so total was the destruction of flesh by fire.

The photographer was in a quandary. Now there was a body found. One dead made this fire no picture for the Newark *Post-Observer*. But if he went back to his office without a picture and later they found two more bodies in the rubble, that would make it a three-fatality fire and that was a picture and he would be chewed out for not getting one.

He was saved from a decision by the fireman who turned over the body. Something under it glittered. It was a golden medal—a narrow trapezoid with a slash mark angling through it.

The photographer took a picture of the medal. No more bodies were found in the fire, but the mystery of the golden medal intrigued the city editor and he ran the picture on page one. No one, police or civilian, had interviewed Lettie Jackson. The corpse was unidentified.

Remo awoke with ths sun shining brightly in his fourth-floor window overlooking the park. He went to the window. He could see the bench where he had spent most of the night sitting and thinking. The trash basket next to the bench was still filled, and he could see a glimpse of the yellow shoes still jammed into the basket. The sight made him feel warm all over. Nothing like a glimpse of beauty to begin a day.

Even though he wasn't hungry and generally ate very little, Remo called room service and ordered a half-dozen scrambled eggs, two rashers of bacon, home fries, toast, and a large pot of coffee. As an afterthought, he ordered a pitcher of bottled water and a bowl of rice, unflavored. And a newspaper.

Was that what normal people had for breakfast? Why not? He had thought about it a lot during the night, and there was no reason he was not a normal person. So, some of his childhood memories had turned sour and a lot of his life had been spent working for a government agency he wasn't too fond of, but he didn't need to be an assassin as Chiun needed to be an assassin. Remo could be a lot of things. He avoided trying to name any of those things.

He had showered by the time the food arrived on a big rolling tray with the newspaper neatly folded alongside his plate. He tipped the bellboy ten dollars, looked longingly at the eggs and bacon and coffee, then put the rice onto his plate and began to chew it tenaciously into a liquid before swallowing it. He opened the newspaper and was startled by a photograph on page one.

It was a photo of a golden medal, and the medal was the symbol of Sinanju—a trapezoid intersected at an angle by a long slash mark.

Quickly, he read the story about a fire gutting a tenement building in the Central Ward. The body that had been found had been identified as that of an unknown woman; the medal was found lying underneath her. The fire was arson, firemen said, because separate fires had begun at four different locations in the building.

A Sinanju medal. But who? And how? He had never seen such a medal, and only he and Chiun knew the Sinanju symbol. Only he and Chiun . . . and . . . perhaps Ruby.

Remo pushed the rice away from him and sat on the bed next to the telephone.

He dialed the number of the Norfield Inn at the New Jersey shore.

When the desk clerk answered, Remo said, "Is the old Oriental gentleman, Mister Chiun, still registered there?"

"Yes," said the clerk. "Shall I ring him?"

"No, no, no," said Remo. "I want you to take him a message."

"Why don't I just ring him and you can give him the message yourself? I just saw him go up to his room."

"Because if you ring his phone, you're going to have one phone crunched into powder. Look, just do it my way. It's worth twenty dollars to you."

The clerk's voice became suspicious. "You going to send it to me over the phone?"

"Chiun will give it to you. Just do what I say. If I

54

have to come down there and deliver something to you, it's not going to be twenty dollars, pal."

"All right," the clerk said disgustedly. "What's the message?"

"Go up and tell Chiun that Remo is on the phone."

"Remo?"

"Yes. Remo. Tell him I'm on the telephone and then when you ring, he'll pick the telephone up without ripping it out of the wall."

"All right," the clerk said. "Hold on."

Three minutes later, he was back on the phone.

"I told him," he said.

"What'd he say?"

"He said something about that he's not no secretary. He's not going to be spending all day talking to people on the telephone. He said Remo who. He said you should write him a letter. He doesn't want to talk to you. He said something about a piece of pig's ear. Stuff like that."

"All right," said Remo. "Now you go upstairs again . . ."

"Wait a minute. How many trips you want for twenty dollars?"

"It's up to fifty dollars," Remo said. "Go back upstairs and tell him that Remo said it's important. It's about Ruby."

"I don't know. He didn't look happy."

"He never looks happy. Fifty dollars."

"Oh, all right." The clerk put down the phone again at the desk."

When he returned, he said, "He says he will make an exception to a long-standing rule and talk to you."

"Good."

"How do I get my fifty dollars?"

"I'll tell Chiun to give it to you."

"I knew it was going to be something like that," the clerk said.

"What's the matter?" Remo asked.

"I saw this Chiun in action yestersay. He came in here for lunch. He ordered water. He wouldn't let anybody sit at the tables next to him. When he left, he walked around all the tables and he picked up the change people left for tips for the waitress. He ain't giving me no fifty dollars."

"Trust me," Remo said. "I'll see that he does."

"All right, but I don't believe it," the clerk said. "Hold on, I'll put you through."

Remo heard the telephone click and then buzz as the room was being called.

The telephone rang a dozen times before Chiun picked it up. As usual he did not speak into the phone, not even to identify himself. He lifted it off the receiver and waited.

"Chiun, this is Remo."

"Remo who?"

"C'mon, Chiun, stop fooling around. Remo."

"I once knew a Remo," said Chiun. "He was an ungrateful wretch. As a matter of fact, his voice even sounded a little like yours. That screeching nasal whine that white people have. Especially Americans."

"Listen, Chiun, I'll wait while you work off your snot, because I've got something important to tell you."

"This other Remo person always said he had important things to tell me also, but when I listened, he told me nonsense."

"Chiun, it's about Ruby."

56

Chuin was silent, waiting for Remo to say more.

"Did you give her a Sinanju medal?"

"No," said Chiun.

"Oh . . ."

"But she had one," Chiun said. "She won it from me in a game of cards. She cheated. I never will forgive that woman."

"A gold medal with the Sinanju emblem on it?"

"Yes."

Remo groaned, a long, anguished *ooooooohhh.*.

"What has happened to my medal?" Chiun asked.

"It's not your medal, it's Ruby. I think she might be dead."

"With my medal?" Chiun said.

"Will you stop worrying about your damned medal?" Remo said. "I told you I think Ruby is dead. They found a body in a fire, a woman's body, and she had a Sinanju medal."

"That's terrible," said Chiun.

"Give the desk clerk fifty dollars," Remo said.

"Certainly. Medals here, fifty dollars there. You must think I'm made of wealth."

"Just do what I say. Give him fifty dollars and hang around there for a while. When I find out more, I'll let you know."

Chiun hung up without answering.

Remo looked at the dead phone for a moment, started to dial another number, then put the telephone down and went back to the breakfast table, where he again read the *Post-Observer*'s story. Arson suspected, but a peculiar kind of arson. Fires started in four different locations, but no sign of tinder or incendiary devices used to torch the blaze.

Remo thought about the location of the fires. It

wasn't vandals. Vandals started one fire and ran. Starting four fires meant a professional job, but who would want to burn down an old tenement? It wasn't like a business, where the owner, after a fire, could claim insurance losses on equipment and goods he had already stolen from the building and sold. But insurance on a Newark tenement fire wouldn't even cover the cost of replacing the doorknobs.

But who? And why?

He went back to the telephone and dialed an 800 area code number. It hooked into a commercial number that advertised a swingers' sex club.

A breathy woman's voice came onto the phone.

"Hi, lover," it said.

"Hello," said Remo to the tape recording. "I'd like to buy a plow."

"If you're as horny as I am," the recorded voice said, "You're probably just throbbing for some company."

"Actually, I was going to watch the 'Partridge Family' reruns," Remo said.

"Listen to this," the recording said. Her voice faded, and there was the sound of a woman breathing hard and a man grunting and the woman hissing, "Don't stop. More, more, more," and as the orgiastic dialogue went on, Remo said clearly into the telephone: "Five, four, three, two, one."

The tape died. Remo heard a buzz and then Dr. Harold W. Smith came onto the line.

"Yes?" he said.

"Smitty, I've got to tell you, I like your new message better than the Dial-a-Prayer I used to have to call."

58

"Oh, it's Remo. What is it?" Smith said. His normally cool voice was chillier than usual.

"Where's Ruby?" asked Remo.

"Don't you know?" Smith said.

"If I knew, would I ask?"

"She's gone. When I got back here yesterday, she wasn't here. I thought you had something to do with it."

"Ruby didn't need me to tell her to split because a place was getting too warm," Remo said. "You haven't heard from her?"

"No."

"Any ideas where she went?"

"She didn't go home to Norfolk," Smith said. "I already checked that."

"Where else would she have gone?" Remo said.

He could almost hear Smith shrug over the telephone. "She could have gone anywhere. She has relatives in Newark. I don't know. Why? Have you decided to come back to work?"

"Not yet," Remo said. There was a sinking feeling in his stomach. More and more he knew that the body found in the fire ruins, charred beyond recognition, was that of Ruby, young and beautiful and vibrant Ruby who wanted nothing more out of life than to live it. For the second time in less than twelve hours, he felt sorrow saturate his body, all the sadder now for being a remembered emotion. The night before, his sorrow had been for himself, for realizing his childhood was gone. But this sorrow was deeper, built on the terrible knowledge that for Ruby all of life was gone. And for the second time in twelve hours, the sorrow gave way to another emotion—anger.

"Smitty," said Remo, "this is important. Do you have anything in your computers about arson?"

"Can I take this to mean you're coming back to work?"

"Please, Smitty, don't bargain with me. What about arson?"

There was a quality in Remo's voice that prompted Smith to say, "What kind of arson? Anything special? Any characteristics?"

"I don't know," Remo said. "Maybe multiple fires started in one building. No signs of fuel or incendiary devices."

Smith said, "Wait." He put Remo on hold.

Remo could picture him putting down the telephone and pressing the button that raised the television console and computer keyboard on his desk. He could see Smith carefully punching into the machine the information he wanted, then sitting back to wait for CURE's giant memory banks to strip themselves, to try to match up what they knew with what Smith requested.

Smith was back on the telephone ninety seconds later.

"There have been five fires like that in the last two months," he said. "First two up in Westchester County. Near here. Then three in North Jersey."

"Make it four now," Remo said. "Any idea who's doing it?"

"No. No witnesses. No clues. Nothing. Why? Why is this so important to you?"

"Because I owe it to somebody," Remo said coldly. "Thanks, Smitty. I'll be in touch."

"Is there anything else you want to tell me?" Smith asked.

"Yeah. Don't worry about Ruby anymore. You can call off your bloodhounds."

"I don't understand," Smith said. "What is this all about?"

"Don't worry about it," Remo said. "We're just doing a favor for a friend."

"Remo," said Smith.

"Yeah?"

"We have no friends," the CURE director said.

"Now we've got one less than that," Remo said.

CHAPTER FIVE

"How long, Lord, how long?"

"How long?" the congregation shouted back.

"How long, Lord, you going to visit this oppression upon us poor black people? Say how long?"

"How long?" the congregation complied.

The Reverend Dr. Horatius Q. Witherspool stood high up in the pulpit overlooking the congregation of 120 persons, 100 women and 20 men past the age of 65. His arms were raised dramatically over his head, his bright white cuffs shooting out from under the sleeves of his black mohair jacket, his gold and diamond cufflinks glittering in the Sunday morning sunlight like day-old junk jewelry.

"We have lost another," he said.

"Amen," said the congregation.

"Fire has again struck and taken one of us away," the Reverend Dr. Witherspool said.

"Taken away," the congregation chanted.

"We do not know who." He paused. "We do not know how. And we have to ask ourselves, was this person ready to meet her maker? Was she ready?"

"Was she ready?" the congregation echoed.

"When they find out who she was, will they find out that she thought of those she left behind?" He looked around and folded his hands together on the edge of the rostrum. He looked over his congregation with his sincere look, which involved tilting his head to the right and slightly squinting his eyes.

"Or will they find that this poor woman left this mortal coil to be with the Great Lord and all she left behind for those who loved her were debts and bills and the eternal footsteps of the creditor? Is that what we will find?"

He looked around.

"We must always remember. When God calls, we want to be ready to meet Him. But we leave others behind. We want to go and meet that Lord, and we want to be able to smile and look that great Lord right in that great Lord's eye, and say, 'Oh, Lord, I has done right by those I left behind. I has left them with the things they need to get on. I has left them with money from the insurance, and when they goes to bury me, they aren't gonna have to sell the furniture or like that, but they will just cash in that insurance policy and they will find the means . . .'" He paused.

"The means," his congregation said.

"'And the wherewithall,'" Witherspool said. He pronounced each syllable very precisely. "Where-with-all."

"Wherewithall," his congregation said.

"'To bury me. And even the church I love, the First Evangelical Abyssinian Apostolic Church of the Good Deal, the Reverend Doctor Horatius Q. Witherspool, Pastor, was remembered in my insurance policy, and they will be able to go right on doing your work, Lord.'"

He looked around again. "And the good Lord is going to say, 'Why, bless you, Sister, and come on right in, because truly you has done my work and shown your kindness and your goodness, and I only wish that everyone would do that, so we could all live together up here in eternity. . . .' "

"In eternity," the congregation chanted.

"In happiness," Witherspool said.

"In happiness," came the echo.

"And with paid-up premiums, to protect our family and our church,' " said Witherspool.

"To protect us, Lord," said the congregation.

"Amen," said Witherspool.

He met his congregation at the back door of the church as they left, pumping their hands with his right hand, and with his left, slipping into their pocket or purse a flyer from the Safety-First Grandslam Insurance Company, explaining how, for a mere seventy cents a day, without medical examination, they could buy $5,000 worth of term insurance on their lives. The flyer also included an application blank, already partially filled out, earmarking $2,500 of the insurance proceeds to the Reverend Dr. Horatius Q. Witherspool, pastor of the First Evangelical Abyssinian Apostolic Church of the Good Deal.

When the last parishioner had left, Witherspool closed the doors and walked back down the aisle of the small church, whistling "We Are Family."

He stopped short in the doorway of the small room behind the altar of the church. There was a white man sitting at the table, looking at the sports section of the *New York News*, where the Reverend Dr. Witherspool had circled the baseball teams he was betting on that day.

The white man looked up. "I wouldn't take the Red Sox," he said. "They're about ready to start their mid-year fold, and laying nine to win five doesn't sound very good."

"Who are you?" Witherspool demanded. He wondered if the white man was from the city's anti-gambling police squad.

"I know how interested you are in insurance," the white man said.

"I don't know what you mean," Witherspool said. He leaned back slightly in the doorway.

The white man stood up and continued talking as if he had not even heard the minister.

"And I represent the 'This Is Your Last Chance, Sucker Insurance Company,' and I have an amazing policy that, for no cash premium at all, guarantees you're going to live."

Witherspool squinted his eyes. He had never heard of an insurance policy like that. "Live?" he asked. "For how long?"

"Long enough to see if those cufflinks tarnish," Remo said. "And the only premium you've got to pay is to tell me who you paid to torch that building down the street."

He smiled. Witherspool did not.

"I don't know what you're talking about," he said. The man was an insurance investigator. He was sure of it.

He insisted he didn't know what the man was talking about. He was still insisting it when he was stuffed into the trunk of a rented car, and even though he was sure the driver could not hear him, he kept shouting that he knew nothing about it for a twenty-minute car ride, until he heard the car pull off the main highway and pass onto a gravel road.

He didn't know what this lunatic was up to, but

66

for God's sakes, didn't he know that mohair wrinkled? And if he got grease on this suit, it was ruined. Five hundred dollars shot to hell. He was going to kick this honkey's ass as soon as he got out of this trunk.

When the lid opened, he blinked once at the noon sun, crawled out of the trunk, and threw an overhand right at the thin white man's head. It missed and he felt himself yanked around and dragged by the collar of his suit, along the ground behind the man.

"You've got no respect at all for clothing," Witherspool said.

"Where you're going," Remo said, "You won't need any."

Witherspool could not move his head, but rolling his eyes right and left, he saw that he was on the grounds of one of the big refineries that bordered the northern part of the New Jersey Turnpike near Newark Airport.

The crazy white man was dragging him toward one of the two-hundred-foot-high stacks that burned off gas waste from the refining process. Up ahead, craning his neck, the minister could see the top of the stack and, high up above, the ever-present flames spitting out the top as they did twenty-four hours a day. Then the white man was at the base of the yellow brick stack, and Witherspool wondered what he was doing. He had little time to wonder because suddenly he was off the ground, and the white man, holding Witherspool in his left hand and using just his right hand and feet, was climbing up the smooth brick sides of the stack.

Witherspool was so frightened, he did not even

67

bother to wonder how the white man was climbing up the smooth, sloping sides of the stack, but he felt the rough bricks against his back, and when he peeked downward, he saw he was already a hundred feet off the ground. And he prayed, really prayed for the first time in years, and he prayed, "Oh, Lord, I don't know what this lunatic wants, but let's make sure, Lord, that he don't lose his climbing skill in no hurry, right now."

A few moments later, Witherspool was at the top of the stack. He could feel the heat from the burning gas fumes. He felt the white man sling him upward and then let go. Witherspool reached out with his hands and caught the edge of the top bricks and was hanging there, his feet kicking into the air below him.

"Don't kick," Remo said. "It makes it harder to hang on."

Witherspool looked up. Remo was sitting on the ledge of the top bricks, as unconcerned as if he were on a park bench.

"I don't like being up here," the minister said. "Take me down."

"Just let go. You'll get down quick enough," Remo said.

Witherspool clutched harder with his fingers. "What do you want?" he said.

"Now, as I was saying, who did you hire as a torch to burn that building?"

"I don't . . ."

"Let me warn you, Reverend Doctor," Remo said. "One more lie from you, and I'm dropping you down the middle of this smokestack. I may do that anyway. Now, who?"

"You bring me down if I tell you?"

He looked imploringly at Remo, who shrugged and said, "I don't know."

"You let me live if I tell you?"

"I don't know," Remo repeated.

"You not drop me down that smokestack?" Witherspool asked.

"I don't know," Remo said.

Witherspool swallowed. His fingers were getting sore and weak, and his stomach was feeling the heat of the stack. "Okay," he said and tried to smile at Remo. "Then we got a deal."

Remo didn't smile back.

"Who?" he repeated.

"His name was Solly."

"Solly what?" asked Remo.

"He didn't say," said Witherspool. "A young white guy. Solly. Maybe twenty-eight years old. He had a partner."

"Who was the partner?"

"I didn't see him, but I heard about him."

"What'd you hear?"

"He's a kid. Like fourteen years old. Solly calls him Sparky and says the kid is a magician at starting fires."

"Where'd you meet this Solly?"

"He contacted me. I put the word out that I was looking for a torch."

"And he contacted you?"

"Right."

"Is he from Newark?" Remo asked.

"I don't think so. I met him in the lounge of the Roberts Hotel."

"Was he staying there?" Remo asked.

"I don't know." Witherspool looked again at Remo, who glared at him.

"Wait," said Witherspool. "He signed for the bar check. He put it on his room. He musta been staying there."

"Thanks, Reverend," Remo said. He pushed himself off the ledge. Slowly, with his back to the bricks of the stack, he began to walk down the smooth side of the chimney. "*Vaya con Dios,*" he said.

"Hey, wait."

Remo stopped. He was ten feet below Witherspool, standing stuck against the side of the chimney as if he were a housefly on a wall.

"What?" Remo asked.

"You can't leave me here."

"Why not?"

"It's not . . . it's not . . . it's not humane."

"That's the biz, sweetheart," Remo said.

He started down again. He had gone another fifteen feet when he stopped and called up to Witherspool.

"Pull yourself up and sit on the ledge. Somebody'll notice you eventually," he said.

"Thanks," said Witherspool. "For nothing. How is this gonna look? A man of the cloth on top of a smokestack?"

"You can always tell them the devil made you do it," Remo said. He moved again down the side of the stack, almost running, seeming to be able to dig his heels into the small cracks between the bricks and using them as if they were broad steps. When he reached the bottom, he turned and waved up at Witherspool, who sat with his ample butt on the brick ledge, trying to keep his rear end from being ignited by the flaming exhaust gases.

As Witherspool watched, Remo walked over to

his car, got inside, and drove off, back onto the New Jersey Turnpike.

He had two stops to make.

The manager carefully explained to Remo that, yes, he knew it was important but, no, he was very sorry, he could not let Remo look at another guest's bill because, well, just because it was against hotel policy and simply could not be done.

Then he sat down in his chair, unable to move, as Remo began to look through all the bills at the Roberts Hotel.

He found one for Solly Solomon. It was the only name that was close.

"This Solly Solomon," Remo asked the manager. "What did he look like?"

The manager tried to work his mouth but could not speak.

"Oh," said Remo. He leaned over from the file cabinet and touched a spot on the manager's neck. He could speak now, even though he could still not move.

"Young guy, maybe thirty, medium height, dark hair."

"He travel with a kid?" Remo asked.

"Yeah. Skinny little kid. Maybe thirteen. Kept lighting matches and dropping them in wastepaper baskets. I think he was retarded."

Remo nodded.

He took all the charge bills from Solly Solomon, put them in a manila envelope, and walked toward the door.

"Hey, wait," the manager said.

"Yes?"

"I can't move. You can't leave me like this."

Remo shook his head. "It'll wear off in fifteen minutes. Relax and enjoy it. You'll feel great when it's over."

Out front, Remo walked to the first yellow cab waiting in line. He leaned in the open window on the passenger's side.

"You go out of town?" he asked the driver.

"If the price is right."

"Rye, New York."

"Too far," the driver said.

"A hundred dollars."

"The price is right," the driver said.

Remo handed him the manila envelope. "This has to be placed in the hands of a Doctor Harold Smith at Folcroft Sanitarium in Rye, New York. You got it?"

"Got it. Must be important."

"Not really."

"Where's my hundred?"

Remo handed him a fresh hundred-dollar bill. While the driver inspected it, Remo looked at the nameplate over the taxi meter. When the driver looked back at Remo, Remo said, "Now, Irving, I know your name and your cab number. If that isn't delivered, I'm going to make your life interesting."

The driver looked at Remo with disdain. His right hand moved instinctively across the seat, toward a stillson wrench he kept there in full view.

"How interesting?" he asked mockingly.

Remo reached both hands in the window and picked up the wrench.

"This interesting," he said. He bent the wrench in both hands. The thick iron handle snapped in half. He dropped both halves on the seat.

72

Irving looked at the wrench, at Remo, and at the wrench again.

He dropped the cab in gear.

"Rye, New York, here I come."

"Doctor Harold W. Smith, Folcroft Sanitarium," Remo said.

"I got it." As an afterthought, Irving said, "It's Sunday. Will he be there?"

"He'll be there," Remo said.

He waited at curbside and watched the cab drive off. Then he walked down to city police headquarters. He stood across the street from the building for a long time. It had not changed since he had walked a police beat in this city and gone in and out of the building several times a day. It had not changed, but Remo had. Where once it had just been an old building with wide steps, now it was different to Remo. He could sense the wear of the steps; he knew how much pressure it would take to crack the stone. He could look at the old brick walls and know within a pound how much force it would take to chip the mortar out from between the blocks. He had remembered a heavy wooden door, but now he saw a wooden door and knew immediately how hard he would have to hit the lock with the heel of his hand to make the door snap open.

He was different. The town had not changed; he had. People said you couldn't go home again, but that wasn't true. You could go home again; it's just that when you got there, you realized it was not your home and never really had been. A man carried his home with him, inside his head, in his knowledge of who he was and what he was.

Remo thought these things and then asked him-

73

self, *but what are you?* And before he allowed himself to answer, he walked across the street and into police headquarters.

Patrolman Calicano was working the police property desk. He was a fixture, implanted in the job by a politically connected uncle, and doing it just well enough that he would be too much trouble to transfer or fire.

Remo stood in front of his desk.

Calicano looked up. For a moment, he seemed to recognize Remo, then looked back down unconcernedly at his papers.

"What can I do for you?" he said.

Remo tossed an FBI identification card bearing the name of Richard Quigley onto the desk.

"FBI," Remo said.

Calicano inspected the card, checked to see that the photo matched Remo's face, then handed the card back.

"FBI, huh? Maybe that's where I seen you. You look kind of familiar."

"Probably," Remo agreed.

"What can I do for you?"

"That fire yesterday. I want to see that medal that was found."

Calicano nodded. He rose heavily from his chair and lumbered to a large wall of pigeonhole boxes. He took a long manila envelope from one of them.

"What's the FBI interested in a fire for?" he asked.

Remo shrugged. "Something to do with taxes. That it?"

Calicano opened the manila envelope, which was perforated with holes and tied in the back with red string.

"Yeah." From the envelope, he took a sheet of paper and a smaller white envelope.

"Have to sign here first," he said.

Remo took a pen and as he started to sign his signature, he couldn't remember the name that was on his FBI identification card. Richard. Richard something. He finally wrote Richard Williams.

Without a glance at it, Calicano put the sheet on the desk and opened the white envelope. He dropped the golden medal out on his hand. He handed it to Remo. Remo took the medal in his right hand and the white envelope in his left.

He looked at the medal. He made a show of bouncing it on his palm. He held it up to the light as if inspecting it for microscopic scratches, then nodded, and as Calicano watched, appeared to drop it back into the white envelope, licked the flap of the envelope, and sealed it tight. He handed it back to the policeman.

"Okay," he said. "That's all I need."

He turned away. Calicano dropped the white envelope back into the large manila envelope, then picked up the white sheet Remo had signed.

He looked at it, then called out, "Hey, Williams."

Remo stopped and turned. "Yeah?"

"I thought your name was Quigley. On your ID," the patrolman said.

Remo nodded. "An old card," he explained. He walked away, leaving the policeman scratching his head and wondering why that Williams, that name and that face, seemed familiar somehow. Like somebody he knew once. But the baseball game was coming on, and Calicano turned on the set and forgot Williams and the medal. Until that night, when he woke in bed, his face contorted like a man

75

who'd seen a ghost. He sat quietly for a moment, listening to his heart beating in his temple, then told himself he was being foolish, that Remo Williams had died many years ago, and promised himself that he would go easy on the linguine with white clam sauce because it always affected him this way.

He lay back and went to sleep with a smile on his face.

CHAPTER SIX

Dr. Smith handed the golden medal to Chiun. The two men stood facing each other across Smith's desk, and though the CURE director was not inordinately tall, he was a full foot taller than the aged Oriental.

"Recognize this?" Smith asked.

Chiun fondled the medal, then quickly slipped it into one of the folds of his voluminous yellow daytime robe.

"It is the symbol of Sinanju," he said.

"Remo said that you gave it to Ruby," Smith said.

"Ah, yes. Remo. And where is he now?" Chiun said.

"That medal was found in a fire. Ruby's dead," said Smith.

"Yes," said Chiun, his face impassive, his voice bland and without emotion.

Smith had seen and heard the look and voice hundreds of times, but still they made him uncomfortable. He knew that he was considered emotionless by the few people who knew him. But Chiun, when he chose to be, could be colder and harder than Smith ever dreamed of being. The CURE director was also suspicious of Chiun's apparent inability to understand CURE and what it did. He was sure that Chiun understood a lot more than he appeared to.

"I think Remo is trying to find the people who were responsible for the fire," Smith said.

"And were people responsible for it?" Chiun asked.

Smith nodded. "It was arson. Remo sent me some information on someone who might have been involved. When we put it through the computers, it turned out that the man involved was the man whose property was first to burn in this string of fires. Solly Martin. We obtained a picture of him from his family, and now Remo has it."

Chiun nodded. Smith felt uncomfortable standing up, but Chiun made him feel awkward about sitting down unless Chiun sat first.

"These fires? They were set for a fee?" Chiun asked.

"Yes, Master," said Smith. "This Martin and a young boy . . . they have been working their way across the country, setting fires for hire." He was surprised to see concern show itself across Chiun's wrinkled face.

"A young boy?"

"We know very little about him, except that he is thirteen or fourteen years old. Why he should be involved with Martin, we don't know. He's not a relative. We've checked that out."

"These fires," Chiun asked. "Are they started in the conventional way?"

Smith looked at Chiun with narrowed eyes. The vertical frown lines over his nose deepened.

"Well, actually, no," he said. "They are unusual because they start without . . ."

"Tinder," Chiun supplied. "And fuel."

Smith nodded. "Why?" he asked. "Is this important?"

"It is important to me," Chiun said. "Where is Remo?"

"I don't know. There's been a string of fires in cities headed west. I gave the list to Remo. He's probably following it. Do you want it?"

Chiun shook his head. "All American cities sound alike to me. New something or some Indian or some saint. I will find Remo on my own."

He walked from the office. As Smith watched him go, he sank into his chair. He wished he had been able to find out why the fact that a child was involved in the arson cases was important.

Chiun paused in the hallway outside Smith's office. He withdrew the gold Sinanju medal from his robes and looked at it with a smile. He flipped it up and down in his hand a few times, as if weighing it, then put it back into his robes.

Then he walked away quickly. This time he was not smiling.

CHAPTER SEVEN

Remo sat in the front seat of his car, folding his map, but every time he folded it, the panel he wanted to look at kept coming up on the inside.

The next stop would be St. Louis. He was sure of it. The fires had been following a pattern, from White Plains to Newark, then city by city, small city by small city, first down the Atlantic coast, and then westward across the country. He looked up and saw a road sign that read 40 miles to St. Louis.

He threw the map out the window into the road-way and stomped on the gas pedal.

In St. Louis, he had no idea where to look to find an arsonist. Did they have hiring halls, like longshoremen? Because he could think of nothing better, he registered at a hotel, then stopped to buy a newspaper, and a headline at the bottom of the page caught his eye.

HOW THE ARSONIST MADE ME
A BETTER PERSON
By Joey Geraghty

Down at Purchkie's Saloon, where my friend Wallace T. McGinty sits for so long that people try to stick spigots in his ear, he was telling me that there are some things that people won't do, even for money. He proved this to me by explaining that he would never think of running a busload of blind nuns off the road into a ditch.

"This is a fact," he said.

I said that he would not know a fact if it bit him in his payment book from Household Finance. Looking around me in Purchkie's Saloon, I said I knew that you could get anybody to do anything, except perhaps to breed wisely.

For some reason, Wallace T. McGinty took this personally. He said we would ask the next person through the door, his opinion would decide, and the loser would buy a drink. Since even a fifty-fifty chance to get Wallace T. McGinty to buy his first drink since Harry S. Truman made the world safe for democracy by incinerating Japanese was a bargain, I agreed.

The first person through the door was Arnold the Matchless, who hangs out in Purchkie's when he is not practicing his profession of turning unsuccessful businesses into urban renewal sites through the application of gasoline and flame.

Arnold got his name when, on his very first job as an arsonist, he forgot to bring matches. He tried to ignite the fire with an electric extension cord and wound up getting a shock that put him in the hospital first and in the state pen second. He remembers the matches now.

"You are asking me," he said, "if there are some things that people will not do for money."

"That is correct," said Wallace T. McGinty.

"Of course there are," said Arnold the Matchless.

"Buy the drink," Wallace T. McGinty told me.

"Wait a minute," I said. "What, for instance, would you not do for money?" I asked Arnold. "Have you ever turned down a job, any job, for cash? I challenge you to say yes."

"Yes," said Arnold, and proceeded to tell me about a mutual friend of ours who was once in the business of horses but whose problem was that he was becoming too famous, especially to the police of the gambling squad when they were not busy taking bribes.

So this mutual friend was arrested for the seventh time and he was going to spend the rest of his life making little ones out of big ones, and he came to Arnold the Matchless with a proposition, because, he said, Arnold was the only one who could save him. He had this wonderful theory that nothing could happen to him if his records were lost. He was referring to his arrest record.

"How can I help you?" said Arnold.

"For a thousand dollars," said our mutual friend.

"What do I have to do?" said Arnold.

"Burn my records," said our mutual friend.

"Where are they?" said Arnold.

"In police headquarters," said our mutual friend.

"Wait a minute," said Arnold. "Let me get this laughably straight. For a thousand bucks you want me to go burn down police headquarters."

"That is correct," said our mutual friend. "You can pick a time when there are not many cops on duty. This will reduce the death toll."

Arnold looked at me and then at my friend, Wallace T. McGinty. "And there you are," he said. "This is a thing I will not do for money, this burning down of police headquarters."

There seeming to be no alternative, I bought Wallace T. McGinty a drink and threw one in for Arnold, too, thereby setting a pattern for the day from which they do not like to deviate.

Arnold the Matchless is like Dracula. He works only at night, and as the sun set over Purchkie's Saloon, he lurched toward the door, his belly filled with my booze, for which I had better be reimbursed.

At the door, he stopped and smiled, blinding me with his only tooth.

"That is why you are never going to be a success in your chosen profession," he said.

"Why is why?" I asked.

"Because you don't ask the right questions," said Arnold.

"What question did I ask wrong?" I said.

"You asked me if I would take money to burn down police headquarters."

"Right," I said. "And you said you wouldn't."

"Correct," said Arnold. He turned back to the door, then stopped again. "But I would have done it for nothing," he said.

This, then, is a notice to everyone I interview from now on. I have given up asking easy questions. Let somebody else buy the drinks.

Remo read the column twice, then found Purchkie's Bar listed in the phone book, and a helpful policeman told him how to get to LaDoux Street.

When Remo got to the bar, there was a television truck in front. A line of people stood outside the bar, and a young man in a Spanish leather jacket and designer jeans was pushing people away from the front door.

Remo walked up to him. "Sorry, pal," the young man said. "The bar won't be open for a couple of hours."

"Why not?" Remo asked.

"Shooting a commercial inside."

"Good," said Remo. He seemed to drift away. The guard turned slightly to chase off someone else, and Remo, watching the guard's eyes, waited until he was turned just enough so Remo was out of his peripheral vision, and Remo moved in behind him and through the door of the saloon.

"Sorry, you can't go in yet," the guard told another man, a workman in plaid jacket and blue jeans by Farmer Brown.

"Why'd you just let that guy in?" the man asked.

"What guy?"

"That skinny guy."

"Go 'way. I chased him, too," the guard said.

"You're a dope."

"Come back in a couple of hours," the guard said.

The old wooden floor of the tavern was criss-crossed with thick electrical cables, and the lighting was as bright as a ballpark at night.

A man was standing at the bar. He was a thick and heavy man, wearing a suit that looked as if it had been mailed to him in a paper bag. Remo recognized him as Joey Geraghty from the picture that had accompanied his column.

Behind Geraghty stood a man and woman, two models dressed neatly to look like customers. Behind the bar stood a bartender, who looked authentic, perhaps because his apron was wet.

Remo sat at a table to watch. The director was standing at the camera, listening to Geraghty complain.

"We ever going to get this done?" Geraghty asked.

"As soon as you get the lines right."

"If I have to drink any more of this slop, I'll puke."

"Don't drink it. Just wet your lips. Now let's try it again."

He nodded to the cameraman, and Geraghty turned around to face the bartender.

The two people next to him started to talk loudly. Canned jukebox music started up. Geraghty began telling the bartender why he thought Shi-ite Muslims were really good people and how the world would be safe in their tender, loving hands.

The director waited until the sound mixer looked up from the tape recorder and nodded that the mix of background sounds was just right. "Now," the director said.

Remo could see Geraghty's shoulders hunch up in tension. He wheeled on the director and whined, "This suit itches. Why do I have to wear this suit?"

"Because it fits in with your image as a man of the people."

"People, my ass. Some people wear Pierre Cardin suits. Why can't I?"

"People who wear Pierre Cardin suits don't drink Bunco beer," the director said.

"Nobody drinks Bunco beer," Geraghty said.

"Come on. Let's just do the commercial and get out of here," the director said. Geraghty turned back to the bar. He began to tell the bartender about the vicious discrimination against the Spanish-speaking in St. Louis. The bartender looked bored.

The director waited for the sound mixer, then said, "Let's do it."

Geraghty slowly turned from the bartender and looked at the camera, as if he were surprised to see it there.

"Hello," he said, "I'm Joey Geraghty." He stopped and looked at the director. "When do I get my check? My agent told me to be sure to get my check."

"I've got it here," the director said. "Now will you do this damn thing?"

"All right," Geraghty said.

They set up again, and when the director called "Move," Geraghty again turned to the camera, again feigned surprise, again said, "Hello, I'm Joey Geraghty, and I'm not an actor, I'm a newspaperman.

"I'm here at Purchkie's Bar with a couple of friends." He waved over his shoulder at the two models behind him, who dutifully smiled at the camera and made believe they were listening to Geraghty.

"I'm making this commercial because they paid me to. But also because who knows more about beer." On cue, the two pseudo-patrons laughed. The bartender tried to smile. He was missing his two front teeth, Remo noticed.

"So let me give it to you straight," Geraghty told the camera, "the way I try to give everything to you." He raised the glass and wet his lips with his beer. Remo could see he kept his lips pressed tightly together. Geraghty reached down and picked up the can from the bar.

"Bunco beer is good beer. That's the way I'd put it." He looked over the director's shoulder at the girl holding the cue cards. "It's a beer for all night. A beer for friends. So when you're spending all night with a friend, drink Bunco beer. Say Bunco and you'll be a winner."

The bartender laughed, and so did the two customers as Geraghty turned back to the bar and again raised the glass of beer to his closed lips.

"Okay," the director yelled, "that's a wrap." Geraghty said, "Thank God," and poured the rest of his beer over the bar. "I hate this stuff. It tastes like horse piss."

He waved at the bartender. "Purchkie, my usual."

Purchkie poured a precise ounce of Courvoisier brandy into a snifter. He put it in front of Geraghty, who swiveled it around in the snifter, smelled it, and said, "Thank Jesus for something a human being can drink." He sipped it and yelled at the director, "Don't forget my check."

He told the bartender, "Purchkie, I'm making you famous."

"You're making me broke," Purchkie said.

"My columns make you famous."

"Famous don't hack it, Joey. You bring me people in here and they don't spend nothing. They just stand around gawking at the regulars. Can't you get me fifteen beer drinkers?"

"The only place you can find fifteen beer drinkers together is in jail," Geraghty said. "Besides, beer drinkers sweat. I'm going to go change."

He left the bar abruptly for the men's room. The camera crew was already dismantling and moving toward the doors. Remo went to the bar. He passed the two models who had been in the commercial.

He heard the woman say, "That Geraghty. What an asshole."

Remo stood at the bar, and when Purchkie appeared, Remo ordered a beer.

"So that's Joey Geraghty?" he said.

Purchkie nodded.

"Good customer?"

"Naaah. I never even seen him in here and then he started writing about the place. He picked it out of a phone book. When he kept doing that, I invited him down. But he don't come much, which is good."

"Why?"

"'Cause I got working people hanging out here. If he hangs out with his fancy French suits and his patent leather booties and his brandy, for Chrissakes, brandy in a snifter, and starts talking about police oppression and civil rights and like that, my good customers'll leave him in a spitoon."

"What about all those people he writes about?" Remo said. "What about Irving the Matchless?"

"He makes that crap up. But I'll tell you. Some people are like real dopes and every day there's a column like that, you watch. I get a dozen guys in here. You can tell they run shirt stores and they're going bust. And they sit at the tables and look around waiting for an arsonist to come talk to them. But they don't drink worth a fart."

"They ever find an arsonist?"

"I don't know," Purchkie said. "Some days, there's a lot of guys coming in with pinstripes. They ain't my regulars. There's a lot of conversations I don't want to know about."

Joey Geraghty returned to the bar, wearing a light gray plaid suit, nipped at the waist, with straight-legged pants. The jacket's lapels were within ⅛ inch of what *Gentleman's Quarterly* had advised would be the season's hottest style. His tie was two inches wide at the base, down from last week's three inches. He looked at Remo.

"What do you think about Islamic destiny?" he asked Remo.

"It's okay," Remo said, "as long as it don't make colored folk uppity."

Geraghty looked at his brandy. "I should've known. In this place."

"What do *you* think about Islamic destiny?" Remo asked.

"I think it's the wave of the future," Geraghty said.

"We all going to march forward to the fifteenth century?" Remo asked.

"You can't judge what a movement is going to be

like after the revolution, when it's in the middle of a revolution."

"When people eat each other, you can be pretty sure they're not going to turn out to be vegetarians," Remo said.

"You're a racist," said Geraghty. He took another sip of his brandy.

"No, I'm not," Remo said. "I just like to be able to tell one wide receiver from another. When they all start calling themselves Mustapha, I'm in trouble."

"Racist," said Geraghty.

"Aren't we all?" said Remo.

"Right. We are. All of us. What's your name?"

"Remo."

"Don't tell me your last name. I don't like last names."

"How about Irving the Matchless?" asked Remo. "He have a last name?"

Geraghty looked defensive. "Sure. Who wants to know?"

"I was just wondering. He come in here?"

"Sure," said Geraghty.

"Introduce us?"

"Well, if he comes in. And if I'm here. But I'm not staying. And he's not usually here today."

And Remo knew the bartender was telling the truth. Irving the Matchless was a figment of Geraghty's imagination.

Remo left a five-dollar tip and took his beer to a table. The bartender had been right. Within a half-hour, the bar, even though it was still before noon, was filling up with nervous men who ordered Chivas on the rocks, didn't drink it, and sat around looking at each other and at the door whenever it opened. Half the men wore hairpieces. The others needed them. Remo wondered if there was a correlation between dwindling retail sales and hair loss. Maybe it came from scratching one's head each month when the bills came due.

A man came in the door. His hair was his own, but his suit looked as if it were on loan from Alcoa Industries. The man looked around the room at the tables.

The men at the tables looked up hopefully like hookers in a Honolulu brothel. Remo stood up and walked over to the man at the door.

"Come talk to me," he said softly.

"Why?"

"Because if you don't, I'm going to fry your eyeballs," Remo said. He took the man's right elbow between his fingers and squeezed.

"Owww. Well, if you put it that way . . ."

"Let's go."

They sat at Remo's table. Remo released the man's elbow, and he ran his hand through his bushy dark hair.

"What's on your mind?" the man said.

"Let's do it just right," said Remo. "One. I'm not a cop. Two. I understand you know something about fire for hire. Three. I want you to talk to me about it."

"Why should I?"

"I thought we settled all that just now," said Remo. "You want me to remind your elbow?"

"All right. What do you want to know?"

"First, how's business?" asked Remo.

"Punk," the man said. "But Geraghty's column always brings out people with things to burn. Everybody around here."

"Okay. Why's business bad?"

"Same thing with my business as theirs. Too much competition. You know, there's only so many shirts you can sell and so many fires you can set."

"I'm looking for a guy named Solly. His last name's Martin but he calls himself something else maybe."

Remo looked at the man's eyes, which blanked out. "Solly? I don't know any Solly."

"He's from out of town. He travels with a kid . . ."

The man's face erupted with interest. "The kid. Sure."

"You know them?"

"No, but I heard about them. They're in town here selling. I heard about them. That's why business is bad. They're taking all kinds of jobs."

"Where'll I find them?" Remo asked.

"I don't know."

Remo looked down at his untouched glass of beer. He picked up a pack of matches and lit one. He used it to light the remaining nineteen matches. The matchbook flared into flame. Remo wrapped his hand around the burning matchbook and extinguished the fire with his palm. "I hoped you'd be more help than that," he said, with sincerity. He dropped the charred matchbook on the table. "So did your elbow."

"Truth, mister, truth. I don't know. I just heard about them. They got into town yesterday, and somehow they been getting to merchants."

Remo waved around the room. "They didn't seem to get to these guys."

"I just heard about them from the grapevine. Solly and Sparky. They're around."

"How can I find them?" asked Remo.

"I don't know."

"Think about it. I'll make it worthwhile," said Remo.

"Yeah? How?"

"I'll leave you with two working elbows," Remo said.

"All right, already. I'll give you a name."

"What's the name?"

"John Barlin."

"Who's he?" Remo asked.

"He owns the Barlin Sports Emporium on Quimby Street. I know he was shopping for a fire. Then when I was going to call him, friends of mine said never mind, he already made his deal with this Solly. Goddamn carpetbaggers."

Remo stood up. "Thanks."

"Thanks for my elbow," the man said.

The Barlin Sports Emporium on Quimby Street was a long, low frame structure with apartments overhead. It was packed into a long block of buildings that all shared the same basic frame building. The sidewalks in front of the store told the story of the neighborhood, littered with dirt, unswept by the merchants. The Sports Emporium and its commercial neighbors had folding extension screens out front, which pulled over at night and locked shut to protect their display windows against vandals. If Remo had been looking for a textbook example of a failing business ready for burning, he realized he could have used the Barlin Sports Emporium.

As he had expected, the owner was not at the emporium. A very helpful clerk told Remo that Mister Barlin had flown to Chicago on business and would be back the next day.

That meant the fire would be tonight, Remo realized.

He decided to kill time by going to the movies. There were three theaters in a row. One was showing "Hong Kong Fury" and "Fists of Steel." The next was showing "Hong Kong Tyranny" and "Fists of Iron." The third was showing "Hong Kong Holocaust" and "Fists of Stone."

Remo saw them all. He regarded it as a very entertaining afternoon and evening. He learned that movies are ninety minutes long, that black men are always millionaires who travel the world doing no apparent work, despite which they own their own apartment buildings and private jets. He found that these same black men, in striving to bring peace and justice to an imperfect world, always join with an Oriental martial arts expert who can beat anyone in the world in hand-to-hand combat, except the black man, because both of them were trained by the Oriental's father. Together they kill a lot of bad people, all of them white and most of them fat. These fat white men are all cowards, corrupt, control the governments wherever they live, and abuse blacks and Orientals. The two heroes also do not like doors, except to kick down while they are flying through the air. They fly a lot.

White women are all prostitutes, lusting after the black man's body. Black women are all noble and they won't give it up, until the end of the movie, and then only because it's true love.

There was a lot of cheering in the theater whenever a white man bit the dust. Remo decided if there was ever going to be peace between the races, all these films would have to be burned first. He wondered if, when he left the theater, he should fly through the air and kick down the front door of the movie house. He decided against it. Symbolic protests were not his cup of tea.

He left the third theater just as it was getting dark. The iron grates had been pulled closed across the front of the Barlin Sports Emporium.

Remo stood in front of the closed store, and when the small line at the theater box office had gone inside and the street was again deserted, he grabbed the padlock on the iron grating between his thumb and index finger. He felt across the surface of the lock for the slightly raised spot under which the tumblers were located. When he found the spot, he squeezed. The top hasp of the lock popped open. Remo quickly removed it from the grate, slid behind the iron fence, and then relocked the grate.

He worked his way to the front door of the store. The lock was a simple double-action deadbolt. Remo looked over his shoulder to make sure no one was watching, then slammed the heel of his hand against the wood near the lock. The door flew open. Remo stepped inside the darkened store, closed the door, and reattached to the door frame the lock receptacle that his blow had loosened.

In the back he found the steps leading to the basement storeroom, and as he expected, the storeroom had shown signs of being cannibalized. It was filled with large cartons and boxes, but the boxes were not filled with sports supplies. They held junk, newspaper, old shoes, broken equipment. What the owner obviously had done, in anticipation of his fire, was to sell off all his equipment. After the fire, he would claim it was all lost in the blaze and file an insurance claim. A double dip.

Remo sat against a box in the dark. For the arson to be a commercial success, the cellar would have to be set afire. It would be the right place to wait for Solly and Sparky; the right place to pay them back for the life they had taken from Ruby Gonzalez.

As he sat there, something gnawed at his mind. There was something he should do; something he should do now. But he could not think of it.

Time slipped by slowly in the dark basement. It had been almost three hours, and Remo realized why: the two arsonists would wait for the theaters down the block to close before they struck. It was just too dangerous to try working in a crowd. He decided to nap, but he had slept only another hour when he heard footsteps overhead. They were soft, almost brushing sounds, but unmistakably footprints.

Only one set. Remo waited and listened, but there was only one person inside the store. The other must be the lookout.

It would make more sense for him to go upstairs. That way, he could get the one in the store, and still have a chance to get outside and get the lookout before he escaped.

He moved silently through the darkness toward the steps leading upstairs.

The boy was laughably small. Remo watched as the youth pulled boxes off shelves and overturned display cases of baseball bats and sports equipment.

"Sloppy," Remo said.

Sparky spun around. He saw Remo in the dim light filtering into the store from outside. Across the street, Remo saw a car parked, with a man inside. That must be Solly. It matched his photo. This was Sparky.

"What do you want?" Sparky said.

"Don't you know yet that the fire should be in the basement to cover the stolen merchandise?" Remo said.

"Don't worry," the boy said. The fright was gone from his voice now. "My fire will get downstairs."

"Not tonight, kid. I'm putting the damper on you," Remo said.

He took a step forward, but then stopped. The boy had raised his arms out to his sides, as if he were doing a Dracula impersonation at a backyard carnival.

Then, before Remo's eyes, the boy began to glow. A blue aura surrounded his frail body. As Remo watched, the colors began to change . . . to purple, to red, to orange, to a brilliant sunny, fiery yellow, and then as Remo moved across the floor toward him, Sparky pointed his hands at Remo, and splashes of flame flew across the room. Remo slid sideways, but he felt the flame brush his clothing. It was burning. He was burning. He dropped to the floor and rolled, trying to put out the fire. He stopped rolling just short of another dart of fire aimed at him by the boy. The clothing fire was out. Remo moved to his feet. But again, there was fire flashing at him. It hit the wooden floor before his feet, and suddenly the floor was ablaze. Flames spat upwards at Remo. He could feel his trousers begin to ignite. The heat seared his face. And there were more fires—he was surrounded by the darts of flame from the boy. He heard Sparky laugh. Remo was surrounded by a circular wall of flame, and it was burning in toward him. He dove though the wall of fire, hit the floor on a roll, and moved behind a counter, where he beat out the flames on his clothing.

He heard the soft thudding around him as flames shot out by the boy hit the walls and the display cases. Everywhere fires flared. Above his head, boxes began to flame, then fell off the shelves onto Remo. His hair was singed. His shirt again caught fire.

He rolled along the floor to put the fire out. Images flashed into his mind. The boy glowing, shooting out flames. How was he doing it? What kind of power was that?

He stood up behind the counter. Sparky was already at the door. Remo saw that he had paled in color from a fiery white-yellow back to a red. Did it mean that he had no more power to throw flame? Before he could move from the counter, Sparky wheeled toward him. He aimed his arms at the ceiling above Remo's head, and then two twin splashes of fire lined their way through the air to the ceiling. As Remo watched, the boy's flame color vanished. Then Remo looked up, just as large chunks of burning ceiling fell toward him. He rolled away. Chunks of burning wood spattered around him. The store sizzled now with the crackle of fire.

There was a smell, too. A bittersweet smell of roast pork, and then Remo realized it was the smell of his flesh where he had been burned.

Had it been this way for Ruby Gonzalez? He heard Sparky laughing as he ran out into the street. Had the last thing she heard been the laughter of that insidious little bastard? Remo, with a growl, jumped over the counter and ran to the open door. Sparky was getting into the car across the street. The man behind the wheel saw Remo coming and quickly threw the car in gear. He drove off down the block. Remo changed his running angle. He knew he could reach the car before it got away.

And then behind him, he heard it.

A scream.

He groaned, stopped, and turned. The flames were pouring through the windows of the Barlin Sports Emporium, licking their way upstairs into the apartments. He knew now what he had been unable to remember in the cellar—something he knew was important. Before Sparky and Solly arrived, he should have cleared the building so no one would be injured in the fire.

He ran back toward the building. The entranceway to the apartments was alongside the store. As he ran up the inside stairs, he could feel his breath coming heavier. He knew that the fire had done damage to his body, but his adrenalin was pumping so hard, he had no chance to find out where. As he ran along the hallways, he kicked open door after door, and shouted "Fire" inside. By the time he reached the top floor, the families were all up. One by one, he made sure that each of them was headed toward the stairway. He checked all the apartments to be sure they had been emptied. Downstairs he heard the klaxon whooping of fire engines. Flames surrounded the building now, burning through the floor from the sporting goods store below.

Remo wanted to answer no questions. He got back down to the second floor, just as firemen were coming in the entranceway. Remo saw them, turned, and ran back down the hall to a rear hallway window. With his fading energy, he kicked out the window and then dove through it, out into the yard two floors below.

He hit the soft grass, rolled over, and then lay still. He was not just angry anymore. He was frightened also.

Up above his head, he heard voices. "Hey! There's somebody in the yard."

"Check it out."

Remo got slowly to his feet and limped off into the darkness.

CHAPTER EIGHT

Remo stopped outside the door of his room. For a fleeting instant, he had felt that there was someone inside, but now as he listened, there was no sound. He heard no breathing, nor the rustle of garments as someone's chest rose and fell from breathing. He put his hands gently on the door, touching the wood with his fingertips, trying to pick up vibrations from inside. There were none.

Reassured, he opened the door and stepped inside the room. He was a wreck and he knew it. The cab driver had not wanted to pick him up. Usually, Remo could convince cab drivers by breaking their door locks and twisting their ears. He was too weak for that tonight. He had paid two hundred dollars cash for the cabbie to bring him to his hotel.

Instinctively, he knew that he must shower and then stop to think this out. He had seen something tonight that he had not known existed, and if he was going to survive it, he had to understand it.

He pushed the door shut behind him and walked across the soft carpet toward the bathroom. He stopped as he heard a voice behind him.

"A disgrace."

Remo wheeled. Chiun sat in the center of the

floor, atop a couch cushion, looking at Remo, shaking his head and clucking.

"Look at you," Chiun said. "Looking like dog doo-doo, acting like a rabbit. Is this what all my training has come to?"

Remo hesitated. Had Chiun been sent by Smith? Was this to be the end of poor Remo? He stayed in position, watching, and then he saw that there was in Chiun none of the intensity Remo had so often seen when Chiun was involved in a mission. The old Oriental sat, fingertips touching across his lap, shaking his head in dismay at Remo's appearance.

"I had some trouble tonight," Remo said.

"Oh. You had some trouble," Chiun said. "I was sure that everything was going wonderfully for you. You look so good."

"Knock it off, Chiun. This hasn't been an easy night."

"And they will get no easier. A fish out of water might not like the first few minutes, but he can be sure that the next minutes will be even worse."

"Please," said Remo. His body, which had withstood the burn of heat and flame, was now paying the price the tension had demanded. Remo felt weak. He could feel his tissues dehydrated and drying. All the fluids he had pushed to the surface of his body to guard against being badly burned were now dissipating throughout his body, and his skin felt parched. His mouth needed water. He could feel a lightness in his head and for a moment, he felt himself swaying to the right. He almost fell, but held himself up by catching onto a dresser with his right hand.

Chiun was at his side. "Fool," he hissed. "Foolish, foolish child."

Remo tried to say something flip, but no words parted his dry lips. He felt himself being steered, almost lifted, because he had no sense of moving his muscles as he was pushed into the bathroom and Chiun was at his side. He left Remo leaning against the sink, turned on the tub water, then helped Remo out of his charred clothing and lifted him, like a baby, into the tub.

"Stay here," he snarled and ran into the room.

"I wasn't going anywhere," Remo mumbled.

Chiun was back in a few seconds with a small stone vial. He took out the curved stone stopper and upended the bottle over the bath water. A thick blue liquid dripped from the bottle into the bath. Chiun stirred it around with his hand, and as Remo felt the liquid touching his body, he felt his skin tingle with a delicate throbbing, almost as if Chiun had introduced the faint electric current of a flashlight battery to the water.

"Not bad," Remo said.

"Fool, fool, fool, fool," said Chiun.

"Not now," Remo said. "I've got a headache."

"You will have more than a headache if this continues," Chiun said and, just as Remo feared, Chiun did not leave the bathroom, but stood over the tub looking down at Remo.

"Don't you know you have obligations?" Chiun said. "You just can't stop killing people because you don't want to kill them anymore. An assassin has responsibilities."

"Let somebody else have them," Remo said. He felt a tiredness coming over him, a wave of sleepiness.

"What would happen if everybody decided he

didn't want to do his job anymore?" Chiun demanded.

"In this country, not much," Remo said softly.

"No?" Chiun said. "Who would roast chestnuts in the streets? Who would fail to teach American children to read or to write to or have good manners if your teachers all walked out of their classrooms tomorrow? If you leave, who will do Emperor Smith's assassinations? Are you going to leave it all to amateurs? Is that what you're telling me?"

"Yes," said Remo.

"That is what's wrong with America today," Chiun said. "No one takes pride in his work. Excuses for assassins wander around blowing up people everywhere, and we all get a bad name. Have you no sense of responsibility at all?"

"Yes, I have," Remo said. "I feel responsible for getting the guys who are behind these fires."

"At least, that is a beginning," Chiun said.

"Because I owe it to Ruby. She was our friend."

Chiun sighed, surrendering momentarily in the face of an intellect that would not respond.

"Doing good is still good," Chiun said, "even if it is done for the wrong reasons."

Remo nodded, although he did not understand what Chiun meant. He was too tired, and then he slipped down into the tub so that the water covered his body up to the neck, and he closed his eyes to sleep. Before he dozed off, the last thing he remembered was a damp face cloth being placed gently on his face, and he sensed the tingle of his skin as it responded to the lotion in the cloth. He thought fleetingly how easy it would be for Chiun just to press his hand down over the washcloth and slide Remo's head under the water and hold him there until he breathed no more, but he put that thought out of his mind as sleep came over him.

Chiun looked at his sleeping student and said softly, "Sleep, my son, because there is much yet to be learned." And then, to watch Remo, to make sure he was well, Chiun sat down carefully on the tiled bathroom floor, folded his arms, and waited.

CHAPTER NINE

Remo did not know how long he slept. When he opened his eyes, Chiun was sitting on the floor of the bathroom.

"You been sitting there?" Remo asked.

"No," said Chiun. "I came in to see if I had dropped something in here."

Remo nodded. Suddenly he realized that the pain was gone from his skin. He lifted his right hand from the water and raised it in front of his face. The redness was gone; where his skin had been scored with thin lines, seemingly ready to crack, the flesh had reabsorbed moisture and filled out again.

"Good stuff you put in the bath," Remo said. "What was it anyway?"

"The eyes of toads," Chiun said. "Ground goat horn. Dried calves' gall bladders." Remo covered his eyes as Chiun went on. "Droppings of water-fowl. Pickled tongue of newt. Salamander organs."

"Stop it, I'm going to heave," Remo said.

"You asked," Chiun said.

"If you were kind, you wouldn't have told me," Remo said. As he started to rise from the tub, Chiun rose and turned his back and Remo was amused at the aged Oriental's modesty. He wrapped a towel around himself. "Was it really all those things?" he asked.

"Get burned again and I'll make you drink it," Chiun sniffed.

He walked out of the bathroom, and when Remo had put of fresh clothes, he came out into the living room. He knew that Chiun was going to try to talk him into rejoining CURE, but he was willing to put up with that, just to be with Chiun again. He had not realized how much he could miss the old scolder.

"I guess you're going to try to talk me into going back to work for Smitty," Remo said.

Chiun was standing at the window, looking out over the St. Louis night sky. Behind him, in the distance, Remo could see the arches crossing the Mississippi River. Chiun waved his hand.

"Do what you want," he said.

"Then why are you here?" Remo asked. Again, for the briefest moment, came the fear that Chiun was here on Smith's orders to eliminate Remo. But that was foolish. Would Chiun have nursed Remo back to health just to kill him? Foolish? Perhaps but Remo knew it might be like Chiun to do that, probably to fulfill some ancient legend of Sinanju that was old before the Wall of China. One never knew.

"Why, Chiun?" Remo asked again.

"I want to know about these fires," Chiun said.

"Somebody's setting fires around the country. They killed Ruby. I want to even the score."

"I know *that*," Chiun said in disgust. "But tell me about these fires. Who is setting them?"

"A man named Solly and a young kid. I met the

kid tonight. Chiun, I've never seen anything like that."

Chiun turned. His hazel eyes seemed to burn into Remo's. He said, "Tell me what happened."

"I found a place they were going to burn up," Remo said. "I went there and I caught the kid in the act. I was trying to get to him . . . Chiun, he started to glow . . . like electricity was passing through him. He was like a human flame thrower. He was across the room, but he just pointed his hands and fires were starting up all around me. Everywhere I turned there was a fire. I couldn't get through to him. When I finally got out, he was gone. I missed him."

"You are fortunate," Chiun said.

Remo sat on the sofa. It was a good hotel, but the sofa slipcover was made of the spun iron that all hotel sofas were made of, impervious to everything but dirt.

"How do you figure that?" he asked. "I've been chasing these guys all across the country and they get away."

"That is why you are fortunate," Chiun said. His hands came out of the folds of his flowing sleeves and waved in the air. Remo had rarely seen him so agitated.

"Are you paying attention?" Chiun demanded.

"Of course I am, but this isn't going to run into one of those long stories, is it?"

"I can tell this one in no more than an hour," Chiun said. "That should be short enough even for you and your limited attention span. Then we will go see the place where this fire was."

"I've got a wonderful idea," Remo said.

"Your having any idea is wonderful," said Chiun.

111

"Talk in the cab," Remo said.

Chiun tried to. Unfortunately, so did the cab driver, who wanted to know why two nice gentlemen wanted to go to that neighborhood, even if one of them was, you know, not American.

Chiun asked Remo, "Is this person in training to be a cutter of hair?"

"I don't know," Remo said. "Why?"

"Why then will he not be quiet?"

"He will," Remo said. He leaned forward and whispered something to the driver, who stopped in mid-sentence.

Remo sat back. Chiun asked, "What did you tell him?"

"I told him you were a homicidal maniac who would visit revenge on seven generations of his family if he didn't shut up."

Chiun nodded as if pleased. "This is a terrible story I am about to tell you," he said.

Remo looked out the window at St. Louis. "They all are," he grumbled.

"This one is even more tragic than all the rest," Chiun said. "It is about Tung-Si, the Lesser."

"Not to be confused with Tung-Si, the Greater, no doubt," Remo said.

"Yes," said Chiun, "but I would appreciate your not interrupting this story with guesses, even if they are correct."

"Yes, Little Father," Remo said.

"Tung-Si the Lesser was the only Master of Sinanju ever to fail," Chiun said.

"He got stiffed on a bill?" Remo asked.

"Excuse me?"

"He didn't get paid? Somebody didn't pay him?"

112

"You are really crass," Chiun said. "All you think about is money. Sit silently and listen."

"Yes, Chiun."

"Tung-Si the Lesser failed. He took upon himself, for the good of the village, a mission and he failed in it. It is for this reason that his name has been erased from the records of Sinanju. Oh, failure."

"How'd you learn about it?" Remo asked.

"Masters have access to other records," Chiun said. "Otherwise we would never learn anything. Anyway, this happened in a land far off from Korea, in what you would now call Mongolia."

"Now we call it Russia," Remo said.

"Yes. It was a very bad time for the village of Sinanju. For many months, the villagers had been sending the children home to the sea because there was no food for them to eat. Nor was there a mission for Tung-Si the Lesser, because the truth is that he was a lazy, slothful man who did not show initiative. Like an American."

Remo grunted.

"And then an assignment came to him from across the sea in Mongolia, and even though Tung-Si the Lesser would rather have stayed in the village, he went on the mission. And never returned," said Chiun.

Remo drummed his fingers on the side window of the cab. St. Louis was ugly. When he had been a young cop in Newark, he had been a pretty good drinker, and since then, looking at cities all over the world, he wondered if city people drank more than country folk in plain response to the ugliness of their environment. Did a drink help you to put up with the ugliness of a city? Then St. Louis would take a barrelful. Two hundred proof. And Newark?

113

His Newark? An ocean of booze. Grain alcohol. Swim in it.

"And he never returned," Remo mumbled.

"He went off to far-off Mongolia," Chiun said.

Remo sighed. "And there he met the people who lived with fire and the fire consumed him and he never came back and that was the end of Tung-Si the Lesser, not to be confused with Tung-Si the Greater. Or even with Tung-Si the Medium," said Remo.

"None of this is funny," Chiun said. "When you are sizzling and splattering suet drops on the floor, you will hope that you listened."

"Sorry," said Remo.

"At any rate, in Mongolia, Tung-Si the Lesser met the people who lived with fire and the fire consumed him and he did not return. But a message did and it told of a battle between the Master and a boy who could create fire out of the air without flame, without fuel, without tapers. And this young boy had been laying waste the countryside, because what else is there to do in Mongolia? And when the Master went to stop him, as was his mission, he was burned by the boy. But he knew of the danger the boy could bring to the people of Sinanju and so, despite his pain, he lingered long enough to write the message to the village and to the Master who would succeed him."

The cab driver pulled to a stop. "Geez, that's a beautiful story," he said.

"Why don't you ride with him?" Remo said. "I can walk."

"We're here," the cabbie said. He pointed to police barricades on the corner by Barlin's Sports Emporium.

114

"Tip this man well," Chiun ordered Remo. "I will finish this tale later."

The fire was out and although it had been water-soaked and gutted, the building still stood. Remo's interference had stopped Sparky from incinerating the building to nothing.

Policemen stood guard outside the building. Water still dribbled from upstairs windows and out from under the doors.

Remo led Chiun through an alley, and they slipped to the rear of the building and then inside through an open door.

"Where did he stand?" Chiun asked in a whisper.

"He was here," Remo said. He pointed to a spot on the old wood floor. Chiun bent down and touched the floor with his fingers. Remo had not had a chance to notice it before, but there were two footprints branded into the floor, as if by hot irons.

"And where were you?" Chiun asked.

Remo backed away about a dozen feet. "I was here."

Chiun turned, as if gauging the distance from himself to Remo.

"And he produced flames across this distance?"

Remo nodded. When he looked down again, he saw the almost perfectly circular ring of fire around where he had stood, where Sparky had started fire after fire. Above him, the beams of the ceiling were visible, charred black and flaking charcoal.

"Let us leave," Chiun said. Without waiting for Remo, he walked out through the shattered front glass of the door. Remo walked out behind him.

Two policemen on duty saw them and spun,

their right hands at their sides, their fingers creeping toward their holsters.

Remo rubbed his eyes.

"Hey, you," the first cop called. "Where you been?"

"We were sleeping," Remo said. "There a fire here?"

"Sure was. Where were you?"

"In the back apartment," Remo said. "We musta slept right through it." As he spoke, he and Chiun kept walking past the policemen toward the corner, where Remo had parked his rental car earlier that day.

"You're lucky you didn't get hurt," one of the policeman said.

"You betcha," Remo said. "I'm hauling my butt tomorrow to a lawyer. Sue the ass off that landlord. You two can be my witnesses."

Remo's suggestion had the effect he expected. The two cops turned away at the threat that they might spend untold hours in court, without pay, as witnesses. "Naaaah," one said. "Don't sue," the other said.

Remo and Chiun turned the corner. Behind them, the policemen looked at each other. After a few seconds, the small, fat one said, "They couldn't have stayed in there without being found. The firemen went through every apartment."

The second cop nodded. "And if they were in an apartment, how come they came out the door of the store? Maybe they were the ones who set the fire. . . ."

The fat one snapped his fingers. "You know, for a change, you're probably right."

They ran toward the corner. When they turned it,

116

Remo and Chiun had gone. They could hear the accelerating roar of a car's motor a block away. They started running, but the car's sound vanished as the vehicle drove off.

Chiun sat in the passenger seat with his arms folded.

"So what did you learn?" Remo asked.

"It is as I feared," Chiun said. "A young boy. The power to create flame from his own body. Untouchable. Unreachable. It is very bad."

"You saying this has something to do with Tung-Si?" Remo asked.

"The Lesser. Yes. The message he sent back to our people while he was dying told of such a boy. The Master told how, when he was burned, he had put the curse of Sinanju upon the boy. And the boy laughed, and he told Tung-Si the Lesser, 'And upon all the Masters of Sinanju, I put *my* curse and my children's children will put their curses.'"

"Come on, Chiun. You don't believe in that. You don't believe in curses."

"I believe in history," Chiun said.

"So what's history?"

"History is the rest of the Master's message. He told of the boy's curse. And the boy said that someday, a young boy of the line of fire people would meet the youngest Master of Sinanju. It would be a battle to the death. And the line of Sinanju would end forever."

Remo took his eyes off the street and glanced over toward Chiun. "He's just a kid," he said.

"And you are the youngest Master of Sinanju," Chiun said, looking stonily ahead.

CHAPTER TEN

Remo let Smith know very clearly that this did not mean he was coming back to work for CURE. That part of his life was in the past, back before he realized what a nice guy he was, but just to show his niceness, he was going to give Smith and CURE a chance to do something good for America by letting them help dispose of the firebugs, Solly and Sparky.

"In other words, you're stumped," Smith said.

"I need some resource help," Remo said, annoyed with his own transparency.

"About what?"

"About people who can set their bodies on fire and then use them to set other things on fire," Remo said. Even as he said it, he realized how unbelievable it sounded. Smith confirmed his judgment.

"That's unbelievable," Smith said.

"Believe it," Remo said. "There are more things in heaven and earth than you ever thought about . . ."

". . . Horatio," Smith completed, "and you messed up the quote. Are you serious?"

"Deadly," Remo said. "I saw it. I got burned myself."

"I don't know then," Smith said. "I'll try to find out something. Where can I reach you?"

Suddenly, Remo was suspicious. Smith was stalling to find out where Remo was. "I'll call you," Remo said.

"That's not sensible," Smith said. "You're in a hurry, I take it."

"Yes."

"Well, suppose I have several people who know something about this. At least let me pick the one that's closest to where you are."

"You do that," Remo said.

"I can't if I don't know where you are."

"Try the Midwest," Remo said, pleased at his cleverness.

"Just where in St. Louis are you?" Smith asked.

"Dammit, Smitty, how'd you know that?"

"I've taken to reading fire reports. There was a fire in St. Louis last night that fit the pattern."

Remo gave him the name of his hotel.

"I'll be back to you as soon as I can." Smith promised.

Remo felt vaguely foolish waiting for the parapsychologist at St. Louis University. He had always regarded parapsychology as kids' games for people with education. In America, university parapsychologists, after what they claimed were controlled laboratory tests, had certified that horses could count and read minds, that unsuccessful Israeli magicians could bend keys and start broken watches with waves sent out over the television set, when almost anyone could start a broken watch by carry-

120

ing it to a television set. Just jarring it by carrying it was enough to start most broken watches, since most of them weren't broken anyway, but had just been overwound.

Remo regarded parapsychology as not much different from psychiatry, except that when you were wrong, no one committed suicide.

He was expecting a little old lady in Earth shoes, carrying a tarot deck, a divining rod, and a headset to listen to the heavenly voices. What he got was a tall, lissome redhead, with the kind of face that would make the heavenly voices wait on line to talk to her.

She smiled at him warmly and waved for him to follow her back into her office.

The woman stood behind her desk. "Won't you sit down?" she told Remo. She was wearing a violet jersey dress, and it clung to her body as if it had developed an attachment for her flesh which, Remo decided, was no difficult matter. The woman's voice was soft, with the musical hint of a laugh in it.

"I'm Doctor Ledore," she said. "I have been told by a scientific foundation in New York City, which provides us with some research funds, that I am to be helpful to you. I am not to ask you any questions. Those are my instructions." She smiled at Remo. "So, of course, I'll violate them. I'm interested in knowing who you are."

"Maybe your ouija board will tell you," Remo said. He realized by the sudden disappearance of her smile that that was not a terribly bright or witty thing to say. "Just kidding," he said lamely.

"Yes," she said. "What is on your mind?"

What was on Remo's mind was Doctor Ledore's

fine chest. He hesitated a moment before remembering what he had wanted to say. "I'm interested in people who are able to set their bodies afire and use them as a torch to set other objects afire," he said.

"Have you ever heard of SHC?" she asked. She sat down behind her desk.

"Yeah, you put it in your car so it stops burning oil," Remo said.

"Not exactly," she said.

"SHC stands for *spontaneous human combustion*," she said. She rose from her seat and walked around the front of the desk. She was close enough for Remo to touch, and he could smell the faint woodsy scent of her perfume. He felt as if she were doing some spontaneous combustion of his body. He looked at her bosom, soft and full in her clinging dress.

"Pay attention," she said sharply, and Remo looked up to see her face. Her words were sharp, but her face was smiling.

"SHC is just what it sounds like," she explained. "A human body burns without apparent cause, and the fire feeds on itself."

Remo shook his head. "That sounds like nonsense," he said.

She walked to a book shelf and pulled down a thick book. "Here's a book on forensic medicine and toxicology," she said. "It was published in 1973, not in the dark ages." She flipped through the book, then handed it over to Remo. There were three pictures of burned human bodies. The caption underneath them said, "Almost total tissue destruction with little involvement of the surroundings."

He nodded and looked up. She said, "SHC isn't some myth, Mister . . . what is your name?"

"Remo."

"It's not a myth, Remo. It's a scientific fact that it happens, but no one knows why. There was a case in Florida almost thirty years ago. Someone went into a woman's apartment. The place was superheated, but there was only one little burn mark on the ceiling. But directly under the place where the flame was seen, firemen found what was left of a body. Ashes, a bone or two and a shrunken skull. Newspapers a foot away from the body weren't even yellowed by the heat, but in the bathroom, a plastic toothbrush had been melted. They investigated it for two years. It's still listed as 'death due to fire of unknown origin.'" She took the book from Remo and returned it to the shelf. He liked to watch her walk. Her legs were long and curvy, and her hair sparkled under the overhead fluorescent lighting.

"It's not nonsense, Remo. It happens. It's happened down through the ages, and we don't know any more about it today than we did then."

She returned to her position in front of him, leaning back against her desk. Arching backward, her pelvis was thrust out toward Remo.

He had to force himself to concentrate on business. "It's interesting," Remo said, "but it's not what I saw . . . I mean, what I'm looking into."

"Which is?"

"Somebody able to ignite his own body, use it as a flamethrower to set other objects afire, then to cool his body down and walk off, without damage to or injury to himself."

"You saw this?"

"Let's just say I know about it," Remo said.

She shook her head. "I've never heard of it," she said. She looked at Remo, and excitement glowed on her face. "Never."

"Trust me," Remo said. "It happens."

She pursed her lips in concentration, and Remo wanted to kiss her. She looked off into space, and he wished she were looking at him.

She raised a finger as if trying to use it to find something. "Maybe . . ." she said. "Let me look." She walked quickly back to the bookshelves. As Remo watched the smooth, flowing lines of her hips and back and thighs, she pooched around from book to book on the long wooden shelf. "Got it," she said. She spun around. Her eyes were electrified.

She held the book open. "This is a book of pseudo-scientific mythology," she said. "Legends, strange reports, never nailed down by scientists. Here's one. It concerns a small group known as fire children. An oral legend thousands of years old. They were able to use their bodies as torches. Apparently, the power was passed from father to son. They laid waste the countryside . . ."

"In Mongolia," Remo interrupted.

She looked up from the book sharply. "Yes. That's correct. How did you know that?"

"I've heard the legend," Remo said. "From the source."

"Then you know as much as I do." She snapped the book closed. "You've really made this day interesting, Remo," she said. She put the book on the desk behind her.

He stood up to face her. "I could make it more interesting," he said. He met her eyes and smiled.

"What exactly did you have in mind?" she said.

"I do parlor tricks," Remo said. "I have extrasensory perception. I can call every one of your little ESP cards without a mistake. Do you love me yet?"

"No. But I could learn to. Can you really do that with the Rhine cards?"

"Sure," said Remo, who wasn't sure what the Rhine cards were.

"We'll see," she said. She took a deck of cards from her desk drawer.

"I've got to warn you," Remo said. "I'm a gambler, and I can only do it when something worthwhile is at stake. What are you willing to risk?" He allowed himself to look at her bosom again.

Doctor Ledore laughed. "I'm sure you'll think of something," she said.

"Yes, I'm sure I will," said Remo. She showed Remo the deck of cards. There were twenty-five cards. Their backs were plain white. On the fronts were either circles, crosses, stars, squares, or wavy lines.

"Look at them," she said. "Five of each kind of marking. Twenty-five cards in all."

"Right," said Remo. "Twenty-five."

"Now, if you were just to guess what a card was, by chance, you'd average five right out of twenty-five. If your score is substantially higher than that, then maybe—just maybe—you have ESP. You want to test?"

"Sure," said Remo. "Shoot."

She shuffled the deck, turned her back to Remo, and laid the twenty-five cards out in a line across her desk.

She turned back.

"Before you start," Remo said, "One thing."

"What?"

"Lock your office door. And tell your secretary no calls."

Doctor Ledore laughed again. She had a free, easy laugh that seemed to find humor where there was no humor. Remo had always found it the mark of the happy person.

But she did as Remo said, then came back and sat behind the desk. She took a pencil and paper.

"All right," she said. "You start from the left and tell me what you think the cards are."

"Am I allowed to touch the backs?" Remo said.

"You can if you wish," the parapsychologist said. "But I wish you wouldn't."

"Why?"

"Because you might be doing some kind of sleight of hand. Touching one card and peeking at another. Misdirecting me."

"Do I look like I'd misdirect you?" Remo said.

"Yes," she said.

"All right, then, I won't touch them." It was still easy. If Remo had been able to touch them, he would have been able to feel through his fingertips the slight impressions that the printing process had made on the thick cards. Not allowed to touch them, he would have to do it by eye.

He moved his chair to the end of the row of cards, so he could look down the entire row. He narrowed his field of vision, until his gaze was virtually tunneled down a narrow tube, ending at the back of the cards. He cleared his mind, to avoid outside influences, even though he found it hard to clear his mind of the scent of Dr. Ledore's perfume.

He called off the cards, one by one.

"Cross, cross, square, circle, star, star, lines,

square, star, circle, lines, lines, square, square, circle, cross, star, square, circle, circle, cross, cross, star, lines, star."

As he called out the cards, the scientist wrote them down on her long yellow pad.

"Done?" she asked.

"Yes."

"Want to change your mind on any of them?"

"No. I'm not sure of the last two, though," he said. "Your perfume kept getting in my eyes."

She laughed and began to turn over the cards, reading aloud Remo's prediction.

"Cross," she read and turned the first card. It was a cross. "Cross," she read again. The next card was a cross. She began to read faster. "Square, circle, star, star . . ." Each card she called was the one she turned over. She looked at Remo in amazement. The first twenty-three were correct. She could not keep the excitement out of her voice. "Twenty four and twenty-five, lines and star," she said.

"Remember, I'm not sure," Remo said.

She turned the cards over. Lines and star. "You could have been," she said. "You were right." She turned and looked at Remo. Amazement was on her face. She shook her head.

"Twenty-five out of twenty-five. I don't believe it. I've never seen anything like that."

"It's going to be your day for surprises," Remo said, as he stood from his chair, put his arms around Doctor Ledore, and pressed his lips to hers.

She was tense for a moment, as if surprised, then her lips yielded and parted, and her tongue darted out to find Remo's. Holding her upright, he carried her toward the couch against the far wall of the room. She pulled her lips back from his. He placed her gently on the couch, and she began to unbutton the jersey dress. "Twenty-five out of twenty-five," she said.

"Forget that," he said.

"I can't," she said. "Is that all you can do?"

It was Remo's turn to laugh.

"No," he said. "That's not all," and he slipped off his clothes and turned to her.

CHAPTER ELEVEN

Remo and Chiun were in a light, breezy park near the foot of the St. Louis arch. Nearby was the Mississippi River, here at least partly clean with the biggest lumps removed, but still an American river, and therefore a body of water whose primary ingredient was toxic waste.

Remo wondered if one day, some river in America would self-destruct and go afire just because its chemical content had passed the tipping point. If so, he hoped that little bastard of a firebug was sitting in the middle of it in a rowboat, fishing.

"Why are you sighing?" Chiun asked. The old man was kicking his silk-slippered feet at pigeons that waddled up to him, looking for a handout of peanuts or bread.

"Because I busted it," Remo said. "Those fire loonies got away, and now I don't have any idea where they are. And now that they know somebody's after them, they'll be holed up out of sight somewhere. How the hell do I find them?"

"Perhaps you are right," Chiun said, kicking at a pigeon. "I cannot argue with your firsthand knowledge of the criminal mind. So perhaps you should just abandon this quest."

"You've forgotten Ruby," Remo said. "This one's for her."

"Ruby would not want you to kill yourself for her," Chiun said.

"No?" said Remo. "That's what you think. That woman was into revenge, and I'm taking it for her. Case closed." He set his lips tightly together and looked out over the park.

"You are just feeling guilty because you disported yourself with that woman this afternoon," Chiun said.

"No, I'm not," said Remo, who was. "How did you know about that?"

"You think after all these years I do not know what you do?" Chiun said.

"Well, anyway, I'm staying after these guys. The question is how do I find them."

"If you insist," Chiun said.

"I insist."

"You assume that they are going into hiding. But they do not necessarily know who you are. They may just simply think you were someone who blundered into their performance. You may just have been an annoyance that they already have totally forgotten."

Chiun kicked at another pigeon, which waddled around at his feet, cooing.

"You may be right, Little Father," said Remo.

"I usually am," Chiun said. "So we must just keep watching for them in places where they can be expected to do business," he said.

"We?" asked Remo.

Chiun nodded. "Yes, we. Did you ever stop to think, Remo, that here, after Ruby's death, you want to do something for her and what it is you want to do is to destroy her killers?"

"Yeah, I've thought of that."

"Doesn't that tell you anything?" Chiun asked.

"Like what?"

"Like this. That you fulfill yourself as an assassin. That this is the only way, in your life, that you will find pride, by doing what you do best."

"I've thought about that," Remo said. "I'm still thinking about it. It's just that I really think I'm a nice person. . . ." He paused, waiting for Chiun to laugh, but the Oriental did not respond. "I think I'm a nice person and *I* can deal with being both a nice person and an assassin. But how can other people deal with that? You think anyone else is going to think I'm a nice person if I tell them I'm an assassin?"

"You are telling me that these other persons, whoever they may be . . . their opinion of you is important to you." He kicked again at a pigeon that had wandered too close to his robe.

"I guess so," Remo said.

"That is a childish attitude," Chiun said. "Somebody has to be an assassin. You were just lucky enough that you were the one who was picked. Think of all the amateurs who try to be assassins and give the art a bad name. And yet you, you of all people, were lucky."

"Some people might not regard it as good luck," Remo said.

"And some people think the world is flat," Chiun said. "You care about these people?"

Remo shook his head. "I don't know, Little Father. I just don't know."

132

"Really, Remo, someone must do something about these pigeons. They are worthless, dirty beasts that neither sing nor beautify the world and yet you Americans feed them fat." Another pigeon was brushing against his robe. Chiun found a peanut under the park bench and with the toe of his slipper pushed it forward. When the pigeon saw the peanut, he moved toward it.

"And as for assassins being nice persons," Chiun said, "why not? I am proudly an assassin. Yet is there anyone nicer than me?" he asked. He stood up from the bench and his right foot lowered toward the pigeon. The flowing folds of Chiun's daytime kimono hid the bird from view, but Remo had caught sight of the bird's last spasm.

He laughed, stood up, and put his arm around Chiun's shoulders.

"No, Little Father," he said, "there is no one nicer than you."

The assistant manager at their hotel apparently thought so, too, because he gestured to Chiun with a large smile when the old man and Remo entered the lobby.

Chiun walked to the man, who whispered in his ear. When Chiun came back, Remo said, "What was it?"

"Something personal," Chiun said.

Remo laughed. "Personal? What personal?"

"My personal," Chiun said. "Please go to the room. I will join you."

"I don't understand this," Remo said.

"'This' then has company. There are so many things you do not understand," Chiun said. He put his hand between Remo's shoulder blades and propelled him toward the elevator.

Remo stepped into a waiting car. As the doors closed, he pressed the OPEN DOOR button. The door opened again, and Remo saw Chiun walking toward a bank of telephones in the far corner of the lobby.

Remo rode upstairs wondering what message it was that would bring Chiun to use a telephone.

Remo was lying on the couch when Chiun returned to the room.

"Why are you lying there, slug-a-bed?" Chiun asked.

"Where would you want me to lie?"

"I would want you on your feet and packing because we are leaving," said Chiun.

"Oh? Just where are we leaving for?"

"New York City."

"That's nice," said Remo. "New York is beautiful in the summer. The heat from the pavement cooks the garbage on the sidewalk and casts sweet perfume over the muggers who are holding a convention on every street corner."

"We are going, nevertheless," Chiun said.

"Why?"

"Because the firemen there are going on . . . what do you call it?"

"I don't know. What are you talking about?"

"What is it when people don't want to work anymore?"

"Public employment," Remo said.

"No. Something else."

"A strike?" suggested Remo.

"That is correct. They are stricken," said Chiun.

"Striking," Remo corrected. "How do you know?"

"I make it my business to be aware of such things," Chiun said. "Anyway, if the firemen there are stricken, then where else . . ."

". . . would our arsonists go?" said Remo.

"Correct," said Chiun.

"On to New York," Remo said.

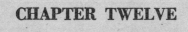

CHAPTER TWELVE

If somebody hadn't put too much oregano in the spaghetti sauce, there might never have been a fireman's strike in New York.

Fireman First Grade Anthony Ziggata was preparing to go from a firehouse in Manhattan's Upper East Side to City Hall to shake hands at the conclusion of contract negotiations. He had showered in the firehouse and was getting ready to put on his dress blues.

Ziggata had been a fireman for twenty-two years. He had last seen the inside of a firehouse as a worker nineteen years before, when he was first elected as a union delegate. He then rose through the ranks to become a member of the contract negotiating team and finally president of the Amalgamated Consortium of Firefighters.

He was in this firehouse only because it was negotiating season, and at least once during every one of the bargaining sessions, one of the New York City newspapers got the original idea to send a photographer to accompany the union president on the job and watch him fight a fire.

This year, the *New York Post* had had that original idea. Fortunately, there had not been a fire alarm pulled in the district, so they settled for a picture of Ziggata cleaning hoses. Ziggata hated fires. They made him nervous, and when he got nervous, his skin broke out in itchy, scaly bumps.

The contract he had been negotiating would cover the city's fire department for the next three years. It would guarantee that the fire department was the highest paid in the world. It did not guarantee that it would be the most efficient. Such suggestions were made only infrequently and tentatively by negotiators for the city administration and were quickly dropped when it appeared that for mere money, the city could buy continuing labor peace. This always appeared to be a good deal to City Hall, especially since the city had gone virtually bankrupt and now depended on Washington and Albany to pay its daily bills.

Everything should have gone simply. Ziggata was whistling. The rest of it was a chip shot—just the formality of shaking hands with the mayor, smiling for photographers, and then he could go home. To his real home. But when he opened his locker, he found his dress blue pants on the floor of the locker.

"Sumbitch," he yelled aloud. 'Who the hell did this?" He held up the wrinkled pants between thumb and index finger as if they were a particularly vile, smelly species of fish.

Nine firemen lay around on cots, waiting for a bell to ring. Like firemen everywhere, they did not talk much to each other, preferring to lie on their cots and listen in to what the others were saying. Since none of the others spoke either, this did not make for much verbal camaraderie.

But they were all together in one thing. They did

not like Ziggata being in their firehouse. Even though it happened only every three years at contract-negotiating time, there was a strong feeling among them that Ziggata might be spying for the city administration, ready to report them for some minor rule infraction. That this had not happened in the last nineteen years wasn't really important; what was important was that it could happen.

"Who did this?" Ziggata yelled again.

"G'wan," came a voice from the end of the room. "If you don't like it, leave."

"Yeah," echoed another voice. "Who asked you here anyway, spy?"

"Spy?" shouted Ziggata. "A spy? Ain't I your legally electoral representative? Ain't I bringing you back a big contract?"

"Yeah, that's what you say. What are you getting out of it?"

"Satisfaction in a job well done," Ziggata said. "I'd like to cut the throat of whoever threw my pants on the floor."

"Go home," yelled another voice. "Wear one of your expensive Guinea suits. You got plenty of them."

"Yeah," said another. "With our money, you got a lot of them."

"Ooooooh," groaned a third as if in real pain. "Why does everybody get fat off us?"

"You're paranoids," Ziggata yelled. "Frigging paranoids."

"Yeah? Well, that don't mean you ain't taking advantage of us."

"Screw you all,' Ziggata said. "If I never see you again, it'll be too soon." He had finished putting on his uniform. He looked as if he had just gotten the jacket out of the dry cleaners and found the pants on a subway platform. "I look like hell," he said.

"Stop worrying about how you look, and try to negotiate us a contract," a fireman yelled.

"What?" screamed Ziggata. "I got us everything we wanted."

"Bullshit," yelled back one of the firemen. He sat up on the edge of his bed. He was wearing an armless undershirt. He had tattoos on both arms from wrist to shoulder. "I got a brother-in-law in Skaneateles, New York," he said.

"Who cares?"

"Yeah? Well, he's a fireman, and they get off the first day of deer season. Paid."

"When the hell is the first day of deer season?" Ziggata asked.

"I don't know but they get it off."

"They get any other holidays off?" Ziggata asked. "Like Christmas or July Fourth?"

"Who the hell cares? They got deer season day. A paid holiday. But they probably got real union leadership."

Ziggata realized it would do no good to explain to the firemen that the fire union had negotiated so many paid holidays for its members that the department's work year was hardly longer than that of public schoolteachers. It wouldn't do any good. His arms were starting to itch. He recognized the signs and tried to calm himself down.

In a final attempt at restoring a spirit of friendship, he went to the pot of food on the stove at the end of the room and dipped out a small helping of spaghetti and sauce. He sat down at the white enamel-topped table in front of the stove, lifted a

140

spoon of spaghetti to his mouth, tasted it, then spat it out. Drops of food and sauce fell all over the front of his pants and jacket.

"Sumbitch," yelled Ziggata. "Who the frig put the frigging oregano in that sauce?" He wiped his spattered mouth on the dirty tablecloth. "Look at me. I look like a pig." He ran to the sink to try to blot himself clean.

"You always look like a pig," shouted back one of the firemen.

"With our money," another one said.

"I hate oregano," Ziggata moaned. "It makes me break out."

"Everything makes you break out. I'm going to use oregano forever," a voice cackled from the corner of the room.

So, itchy, bumpy, skin scaly Anthony Ziggata reached the mayor's office at City Hall and was not in a good mood and when the mayor smiled at him, waved across the room, and walked up to shake his hand and asked, "How'm I doing," Ziggata said, "You're doing shit."

"What's wrong?" the mayor asked.

"We ain't got no deal unless we get deer season day off."

"Deer what?"

"Deer season day. It's the first day of deer season."

"When is it?" the mayor asked.

"I don't know," Ziggata said. "Ask a frigging deer. I ain't no frigging deer."

"Why do you want it off?"

Ziggata took a deep breath. "There is a large hue and cry among the men of our valiant department for deer season day off as a paid holiday to bring

141

us parity with the vast majority of other fire departments across the breadth and depth and longitude of the United States."

"You already have sixty-three paid holidays," the mayor sputtered.

"Well, make it sixty-four. Deer day or we walk," Ziggata said.

"Walk," the mayor said. It was the first time in twenty years that the occupant of the New York City mayor's office hadn't knuckled under to a threat. The mayor was surprised to look around and find that the clocks hadn't stopped, the sun had not stopped moving, and the walls of the building were still intact. He felt exhilarated. Probably, there were mayors and public officials around the country who said no once, maybe even two or three times a year. He bet they liked doing it. It was like having power.

He yelled at Ziggata's back. "No, dammit. I say no, no, a thousand times no. I'd rather die than say yes."

And so Anthony Ziggata, in a funk over the oregano sauce stains on his blue uniform, his skin itching, went out to the waiting reporters and called the city administration and specifically the mayor a gang of fascist, racist oppressors and repressors intent upon breaking the spirit of true trade unionism in America. And he said that if the firemen were expected to be ready to die for the city, as so many did, they were also ready to die for their honor, and the mayor had not heard the last of this.

By the time the stories had reached the firehouses of the city, they had been changed somewhat. The firemen "learned" that the city police had demanded in their next contract that each policeman be paid three times what a fireman was paid, since they worked three times as hard. By unanimous voice vote, every fire company in the city authorized Ziggata to call a strike to hold off the rampaging police union plunderers. Ziggata by now had on a fresh pair of pants, and a bath had gotten rid of most of the itching, and he was home in Ozone Park, Queens, and he didn't want to hear from strike. But when he got the first of many phone calls calling him a traitor to the firemen's cause and warning him that he might forfeit the 125 percent of salary pension all firemen were entitled to after completing ten years of more or less loyal service, he did the only thing a self-respecting union man could do.

He brought the department out on strike.

Soon after, Solly and Sparky arrived.

CHAPTER THIRTEEN

The mayor had set up a crisis headquarters in City Hall, and when he arrived there after eating Szechuan food in Chinatown, he asked a woman outside City Hall, "How'm I doing?" She hit him on the head with her umbrella. He arrived at the crisis center shaken, careful enough to ask his aide, "How are *you* doing?"

"Terrible," his top aide said. He was a swarthy Latin-looking man with a rumpled suit and a greasy tie who wanted to stay in office just long enough to buy a restaurant. "Goddam, alarm boxes are going off all over the city, and nobody's answering them."

"What's burning?"

"Nothing yet. They're all false alarms."

"You sound like you've got it under control. I'm going out to mingle," the mayor said. He had been out of the building only a few minutes when the fires started.

Solly Martin and Sparky McGurl drove through New York's nighttime streets. They headed east down 81st Street.

"This block'd go in minutes," Martin said. The

boy didn't answer, and Solly looked over at him. The kid had a book of matches and a paper bag that their pastrami sandwiches had come in. He was tearing strips of paper from the bag, lighting them and tossing them out the car's open window.

"Stop that," Solly growled.

The kid looked at him, first with a flash of anger, then turning it to a smile. "Just practicing, Solly," he said.

"You don't need any practice."

The kid kept smiling. "No, I guess I don't."

"And besides, you burn nothing without a contract," Solly said.

"*You* don't," the boy corrected. But he put the bag and the matches back into the glove compartment.

Solly looked back into the street, in time to swerve to avoid a big Gordon setter who seemed intent on proving that sexual intercourse between dog and parked car was possible. The kid was changing. He had been hanging on Solly like a father or a big brother, but now he had the look of somebody ready to spread his wings and go on his own. The kid hadn't been the same since the fire in St. Louis.

"Still thinking about that guy?" Martin asked him.

"Yeah," Sparky said. "I don't know. When I saw him, first I was scared. But then it was like I'd been waiting for him. Like I was always waiting for him."

"You ever see him before?" Martin asked.

The kid looked out the window and shook his head. "No. I mean, not really. But it's like he was familiar, you know, like I seen him before but

146

didn't really see him, like, you know what I mean."

"No."

"It's like I lived before and so did he, and like, we were supposed to meet because like we had an appointment. It was weird."

"Well, we're rid of him. Never see him again," Solly said.

Sparky shook his head in disagreement. "I don't think so," he said. "I don't think so."

Solly was glad they were back in New York. The kid was acting strangely. But this firemen's strike was made to order for them. One big score and Solly would retire, and the kid could spend the rest of his life setting fire to supermarket carts for all Solly cared.

The fires started in Harlem, where groups of teenagers decided that the way to improve the quality of their housing was to live in the street, so they began to torch their own apartment buildings.

Soon dozens of buildings were ablaze. In the absence of a fire department, policemen were trying to man fire equipment and fight the fires, after first extorting from the mayor a promise of triple time for overtime. The same youths who had set many of the fires were pitching in, trying to put them out.

The reports crackled in over the all-news radio station in Solly Martin's car.

Solly swore.

He and Sparky were driving down what was left of the West Side Highway. The problem with driving this high-speed elevated thoroughfare was that a driver had to get off the road every six or eight blocks as he came to a section of the road that was

147

sealed off because it was falling apart. Solly drove down to 11th Avenue, drove at street level for a few blocks, then was able to get back up on the West Side Highway.

They were moving south along the Hudson River toward downtown. Solly swore again at the radio.

"Goddamn amateurs," he said. "There won't be anything left for us to burn, if they keep it up."

Sparky smiled and pointed out the window, straight ahead, toward downtown. "There's something that belongs to us," he said.

Solly followed the direction of the kid's gesture. He smiled, too, as he saw what Sparky meant.

The twin towers of the World Trade Center, the tallest buildings in New York City, jutted up into the sky like two upended silvery packs of gum.

"They're fireproof," Solly said.

"Not to me. I can make anything burn."

"Kid. I think you got it."

The mayor came back to crisis control center shaken. His city was burning up. From Harlem in the north to Chinatown on the south, from river to river, fires were exploding all over the city. The mayor had called on the state to mobilize and send in the National Guard; he had authorized police overtime to man fire equipment; he had called on private citizens to form bucket brigades to help fight fires. He had tried to call in the sanitation workers, too, but their leader had asked the mayor how much he expected a garbageman to do for $29,000 a year. The mayor had to promise them quadruple time before the union leader said grudgingly that he would tell the men and let them decide themselves.

148

"Maybe I should call the teacher's union," the mayor said.

His aide shook his head.

"Why not?"

"They won't even give out milk in classrooms. You think they're going to fight fires?"

"It might be a welcome change from not teaching," the mayor said.

"You're wasting your time," his aide said. "Try the governor again about the National Guard."

A commissioner of the agency that built and operated the World Trade Center pushed his way into crisis central.

The mayor saw him and smiled. "How'm I doing?" he asked.

"We're doing terrible," the commissioner said. "All of us. We've got to talk."

"Over here," the mayor said. His aide watched as the two men went to the side of the room. He walked over to join their conversation.

"I just talked to some guy on the phone," the commissioner said. He was a balding, sweaty man. "He's going to burn down the World Trade Center."

"There's always an unless," the mayor said. "What's the unless?"

"Ten million dollars. That's what he wants."

"What do you think?" the mayor asked. "Probably a crank."

"I don't know what to think. I don't think he was a crank."

"You want to pay him?" the mayor asked.

"Where am I going to get ten million dollars?"

The mayor laughed. With a stranglehold on the revenues of all bridges and tunnels leading into and out of the city, the economy of the World Trade Agency was as sure as Saudi oil reserves.

"Raise tolls again," the mayor said. "What do you want me to do?"

The commissioner kept rubbing his hands together as if trying to wash them of some psychic dirt. "Protect our buildings. They're not paid for yet."

"Sure," the mayor said. "What do you want? I've got six Boy Scout troops I can mobilize. Maybe the League of Women Voters will come out. They can carry water in their pocketbooks."

He was interrupted by his aide. "Mayor, I think you ought to take this call."

The mayor nodded. "Wait," he told the commissioner.

He picked up the telephone and pressed a button. "This is the mayor," he said. He listened and said, "But you can't do that." He looked at the two men standing in the corner and shook his head. Then he looked at the telephone, as it obviously had gone dead in his hand.

He came back and *whooshed* a large sigh. "That was your arsonist," he told the commissioner. "He said he knew I must have heard about it by now. Ten million dollars or the twin towers get melted."

The aide said, "Can he do it? I thought those buildings were fireproof."

"He said he can do it," the mayor said. "Get the police over to the Eastern Marine Terminal on FDR Drive," the mayor said.

"Why?"

"He said that's a fireproof building, too, and he's putting it up, just to show us he can do it."

The aide raced to a telephone, picked it up, and began talking.

The commissioner shook his head. "You've got to settle this strike," he told the mayor.

"Sure. Give them off the first day of deer-hunting season?"

"Give them any goddamn thing they want," the commissioner said. "This is big."

"You going to give your cops deer season off?" the mayor asked.

"They haven't asked for it. But you've got to," the commissioner said. He wiped his brow with a wet handkerchief. "This is important."

"Some things are more important," the mayor said. He looked toward his aide, who put the telephone down slowly as if not believing the message it had brought him.

He came back, his face drained of color.

"The worst?" the mayor said.

"Yeah," said the aide. "We were too late. The police said the Marine Terminal's rubble. It went up like a match, and the flames were so hot, it's like the stones almost melted. Five, maybe six, dead inside."

"Give in," said the commissioner. "Give in. Settle."

"Get out of here," the mayor said. "You make me sick."

As the night wore on toward midnight, fires were blossoming all over the city, and as Remo and Chiun's plane angled in toward John F. Kennedy Airport, they could seem the sky glowing over the city.

In a rented car, driving into Manhattan, Remo listened to the news bulletins on the radio:

• The National Guard was moving in, the governor authorizing it after finally having been located at the opening of a new Beautiful People disco.

• The mayor was asking the public to mobilize and help fight the fires in the city. "I know they will respond," he said.

• The press did not know why, but the twin towers of the World Trade Center had been sealed off by agency police. All train service into the building had been stopped, and no one was being allowed into the area housing the mammoth structures.

"What do we do now?" Chiun asked.

"The mayor's at City Hall," Remo said. "We're going there. It looks like the World Trade Center is on Sparky's hit list."

CHAPTER FOURTEEN

The kid had flipped. Solly Martin knew it when he had to drag the young boy out of the blazing East Side Marine Terminal. The building was falling around him; there were the screams of the burning and dying, and Sparky McGurl had wanted to stay there and wait for the cops to arrive so he could incinerate them, too. When Solly had dragged him back to the car, the kid's eyes were flashing with excitement. The excitement of death.

Martin drove instantly downtown, then through the Holland Tunnel from New York into Jersey City. They made a left hand turn near the Holiday Inn, then headed south toward the decaying heart of the old city.

At burned-out City Hall, they made another left-hand turn and drove back toward the water, toward the Hudson River and the New York skyline.

Exchange Place, busy during the day with the work of responsible stock firms and a handful of boiler rooms that specialized in selling worthless stock over the telephone to people who shouldn't even have been allowed to have a telephone, was dark and empty. They parked their car against a wooden timber that acted as a retaining wall to prevent cars from rolling into the murky waters of the Hudson, here so decayed and volatile that they could have peeled off a car's paint before it touched the mud of the shallow bottom.

"What are we doing here?" Sparky asked. His voice was annoyed and demanding.

"Leave it to me," Solly said. He took a flashlight and a screwdriver from under the front seat, jammed them into his belt, then both left their car.

A wooden kiosk marked the entrance to the Port Authority Trans-Hudson subway, which went under the river from his spot in New Jersey to New York. The subway station, in keeping with the Port Authority's commitment to equality for New Jersey, was possibly the dirtiest and ugliest in the United States. Going down into it gave the impression of entering a coal mine.

The kiosk door was locked. A sign posted read:
ALL TRAIN SERVICE CANCELLED.

TRAINS TO NEWARK AT JOURNAL SQUARE.

Solly peered in through the dirt-crusted window. The building was dark. The old metal and wood door pulled open easily after Solly stuck the screwdriver into the lock. They both stepped into the darkness.

They stopped to listen, and when they heard no sound, Solly flipped on his flashlight for a brief instant. He saw the steps leading down at the end of the long entrance hallway.

"Follow me," he whispered. "And be quiet."

They walked down three flights of steps, pausing at every landing to listen, and then they were in another long hallway. At the end of it, Solly saw the turnstiles marking the entrance to the tubes. The Port Authority indicated its priorities by hav-

155

ing kept the turnstiles still working, the faint red glow from their automatic coin-demanders creating an eerie halo around the entranceway. Solly and the boy slid under the turnstile, and Solly again flipped on his light. He saw a sign that read: WTC—WORLD TRADE CENTER—and they turned right, down another flight of stairs. They were on a subway platform. They paused, listening.

When he was sure the platform was empty, Solly led the youth to the edge of the platform. He flashed his light as they jumped down onto the wooden timbers that transversed the tracks. They began to walk to the left.

Solly leaned over to the boy. "Next stop, World Trade Center," he said. The boy giggled as they walked off in the dark into the tunnel that led under the Hudson River to the twin towers in New York.

A New York City police squad of two captains, three lieutenants, and four sergeants, all supervising one patrolman, stood guard outside the crisis control center in the City Hall building.

The patrolman stood at the door. The nine superior officers sat in chairs, watching him carefully for even the smallest hint of inefficiency or insubordination.

The patrolman stopped Remo and Chiun when they appeared at the door. Remo showed his FBI identification.

The patrolman looked at it, then called toward the group of sergeants.

"Sir?"

The sergeant with the least seniority came over. "Yes, patrolman?"

"This man's from the FBI. Here's his identification."

The sergeant fondled it. He nodded several times, then took it back to the other sergeants. He showed it to the sergeant with the next most seniority, who fondled the ID, nodded, and passed it on to the senior sergeant. The three sergeants huddled. They took turns fondling the ID card. Finally, the lowest-seniority sergeant carried the card to the lieutenant with the least seniority.

"Hey," Remo called. "Is this almost a wrap?"

"Procedures," the ranking sergeant called. "They have to be followed."

The lieutenants were now in heated discussion, apparently deciding who was going to take the FBI card to the two captains for evaluation.

Remo walked over to the three lieutenants and took the card back. He motioned for the four sergeants to join him. He motioned for the two captains to come over. When all nine had assembled, he held up the card.

"This is an FBI card. It belongs to me. The Oriental gentleman is with me. We are on government business. We are going inside."

"Do you have approval?" one of the captains said.

"I do now," Remo said. He put the card back into his shirt pocket. His hands flashed in the air. Later, the patrolman would say that he hadn't seen anything, but suddenly all nine officers were holding their faces. Their noses hurt.

"That's just a touch," Remo said. "You understand. Now I've got approval, right?"

"Right," said nine voices.

"Thank you."

Remo went back to Chiun. The patrolman moved aside.

"We've got approval," Remo said.

The patrolman winked.

Inside the room, the mayor sat with his head resting on his hands, as if trying to wring a headache out of it.

"Another string of fires, up along York Avenue," his aide called to him.

The mayor shook his head. "Call the firemen. Tell them to go back to work."

The aide said, "You can't do that. It'll kill you politically."

"And if I don't, there are going to be bodies stacked up all over this city," the mayor said. "Tell them they can have deer season off. They can have duck season. They can have frigging mongoose season. I'm gonna get their asses later, but they've got to go back."

The aide started to protest, but the mayor barked, "Do it." Then he looked up and saw Remo.

"What do you want?" he asked.

"What's the ransom demand on the World Trade Center?" Remo asked.

"Ten million dollars."

"You going to pay it?" Remo asked.

"No. I'm waiting for them to lower their demand to deer season off. *That* I can give them."

"Is the Trade Center agency going to give them the money?"

"No," the mayor said. "Who are you, anyway?"

"I'm from Washington," Remo said. "This is my assistant." He nodded toward Chiun. Chiun glared at him.

"I am his teacher," Chiun corrected. "Everything he knows I taught him. Except how to be ugly. He came by that naturally."

"You sound like my mother," said the mayor.

"I bet you never write her," Chiun said.

"Will you two stop?" Remo said. "We've got business. The arsonists are going to call back?"

"Yes," the mayor said.

"When those firemen go back to work, you're still going to have a problem."

"What's that?"

"Those arsonists. They really can burn down the World Trade Center. They can burn down this whole city."

"What's left of it, you mean," said the mayor.

"Right. What's left of it. Anyway, if you don't stop them, this city is in bad trouble and going to stay in bad trouble."

"As opposed to?" the mayor asked.

"When are the arsonists calling back?"

The mayor looked at the wall clock. "Five minutes," he said.

The aide interrupted him. "Mayor, I just talked to the firemen."

"Yes?"

"They want St. Swithin's Day off, too."

"What the hell is St. Swithin's Day?" the mayor asked.

"I don't know, something about a groundhog, I think," the aide said.

"No," the mayor said. "It's rain. Groundhog is winter or something." He groaned again. "Give it to them. Give them anything. It doesn't matter. I'm gonna have all those bastards thrown off the frigging department if it's the last thing I do."

The aide nodded and went back to the phone. Remo said, "All right, Mayor, when the arsonists call, here's what you do."

CHAPTER FIFTEEN

The Trade Center police still ringed the block, but all of them had been pulled out from inside the twin tower complex when Remo and Chiun arrived. The lights had been turned out in the lobby, but as the two men walked down the store-lined corridor connecting the two towers, a flashlight beam shone from one end into their faces.

"Who are you?" a voice called.

"I can't hear you," Remo said. "I've got a flashlight in my face."

The light went out. "One man only," Chiun hissed to Remo.

"Now who are you?"

"I've got your money," Remo said. He swung the attaché case he was carrying into the air above his head before realizing that his questioner couldn't see it in the dark. Remo made out the man. Early thirties, flashily dressed, wearing two gold rings. He had seen him before behind the wheel of a car in St. Louis. Solly Martin. Remo was disappointed. He had hoped that the kid Sparky would be here, too.

Remo and Chiun walked toward him. Solly's voice was crisp.

"That's far enough," he said.

"We're twenty feet apart," Remo said. "How do I get you your money unless we get closer than that? Mail it?"

"What's the money in?"

"A briefcase," Remo said.

"Okay. Put it down on the floor, then back up."

The light flashed on. Remo put down the attaché case and then motioned for Chiun to back away. So did Remo.

They saw the flashlight click on, zero in on the attaché case, and then come closer. It waved up to them.

"Back farther," Solly called. "No funny stuff. I've got a gun on you."

"No gun," Chiun whispered to Remo.

"How do you know?"

"His balance when he walks. He is just one flashlight off in balance. Not a flashlight *and* a gun," Chiun said.

Remo had made the same judgment. "Maybe he's dragging the gun on a rope behind him," he said sullenly.

"No," Chiun said thoughtfully. "I don't hear that."

The flashlight was at the attaché case. Solly bent down to flip it open.

Remo said, "Where's Santa's little helper?"

"Sparky? He's upstairs ready to put this building away if there's any funny stuff." Suddenly, he realized that no one should have known about his young accomplice. He looked up at Remo as he fumbled with the locks. "What do you know about . . ."

Remo interrupted. "You set many fires?"

"Enough to know what we're doing," Solly said.

"Who are you?"

"You set that one in Newark? At the tenement? For Reverend Witherspool?"

"Yeah. That was ours. Good fire."

In the dark, Remo nodded. "A friend of ours died in that fire."

"Sorry to hear it," Solly Martin said. "That's life."

"I'm glad you're taking that attitude," Remo said.

Solly had forgotten the question he asked Remo in his hurry to get the case of money open. He lifted the top, glanced at the money, then raised his light toward Remo, catching him full in the eyes. Remo saw the swing of the light and contracted the pupils of his eyes before the light hit him, and when the light was on him, the pupils of his eyes were only little pinpricks of black.

"I know you from somewhere?" Solly asked. He rotated the light around Remo's face.

"We never met," Remo said. "But we almost did in St. Louis. At the sporting goods store."

"That was you?"

"Yeah."

"You spooked the kid."

"Nothing compared to what I'm going to do," said Remo.

"What do you mean?"

"I mean, you're first and then him. That's phoney money there. It's just cut-up newspaper, under a few bills. Phoney stacks."

The light swung down toward the attaché case, but before Solly Martin could even glance at the money, Remo was on him, his right hand like a claw around the back of Martin's neck.

"Where's the kid?" Remo asked.

164

"I don't know. Owwwww. I don't know."

"What do you mean, you don't know?"

"He's upstairs somewhere. In this building."

"And how's he going to know you've got the money?" Remo asked.

"He's going to call me on that phone over there." Solly tried, ineffectively, to point to a pay phone on the wall.

"Is that the truth?" Remo asked, even though he knew it was. Pain in judicious doses, judiciously applied, always brought the truth, and Remo was a master at the measured dose of pain.

"Yeah, it's the truth," Solly said. "This is a shit deal."

"Maybe you're in the wrong business," Remo said.

"I was always in the wrong business. And here, finally, I thought I had it. And now . . . goddamn jail."

Remo shook his head. In the glow from the flashlight, forgotten on the floor, Solly could see Remo's face, the dark, deep-set eyes, the high cheekbones, and a shiver went through the man's body.

"What do you mean, no?" he asked. "You're a cop, ain't you?"

"Sorry, kid. Not me. I'm an assassin."

"Hear, hear," said Chiun. "And about time, too."

"What's next?" said Solly nervously. His voice trembled.

"You are. Good-bye, Solly," said Remo.

"You're going to kill me?"

"For a friend named Ruby," Remo said.

"You can't do that," said Solly.

"Watch," said Remo.

165

As he finished Solly, the telephone on the wall rang. Before Remo could move toward it, Chiun had lifted the receiver.

"Chiun," hissed Remo. "I'll handle that."

"Just a minute," Chiun said into the phone. "Remo wants to talk to you." He handed the telephone to Remo. Remo glared at him.

"Kid?" said Remo.

"Yeah?"

"Solly's here. He's got the money."

"Good. Let me talk to him."

"He says hurry on down."

"If I don't talk to him, I go to work."

Remo moved close to the mouthpiece, as if whispering. "Kid, you better get down here. I think he's planning to take a walk with your money."

Sparky laughed, a chilling, hollow laugh that pierced Remo's hearing. "Who cares?" he said. "Let him keep the money. I just want to burn."

"You're not gonna burn, wiseass," said Remo. "You're gonna fry."

The kid paused, then said, "I know you."

"St. Louis," said Remo.

The young boy laughed again. "I knew you'd be along," he said. "It makes it right sort of."

"You think so?" Remo asked.

"Yeah. It's like I been waiting my whole life for you. Like we got some kind of business, you know, like that."

"We've got business, kid," said Remo. "It's been hanging around for thirty centuries."

"Ninety-second floor," the kid said. "I'll be waiting for you."

"You got it," Remo said. He let the telephone go dead in his hand, then turned to Chiun with a

166

quizzical look on his face. "He said he's waiting for me."

"I heard what he said," said Chiun, who was standing ten feet away. "Do you think I'm deaf?"

"He knows the legend, too," Remo said.

"Everyone knows it and believes it but you," said Chiun.

Remo put his hand on Chiun's shoulder. "Little Father," he said. "Me, too."

He walked toward a bank of elevators with Chiun at his side. Remo studied the elevator signs in the lobby. There was no elevator to the 92nd floor. They only went as high as the 60th floor. They started to ride up in the silent building.

"I hate this," Remo said.

"What?"

"You can tell a country's gone to hell when they start messing around with elevators."

"This one seems to work fine," Chiun said.

"Naaah," said Remo. "You know, in the old days, elevators used to go from the bottom floor to the top floor. Whoosh. Straight up. Now, they got classes in engineering schools in creative elevator design. They go halfway up. Others go a quarter of the way up. When you get there, you have to get a schedule and switch elevators like switching trains. Trying to get to the top floor is like trying to get to Altoona to see Aunt Alice. Stupid."

"I didn't know you knew so much about elevators," Chiun said.

"Just the way I am," said Remo. "I know a lot about so many things."

"Then here is something you should know," Chiun said. He was interrupted by the elevator door opening. They stepped out and transferred to

167

another elevator. It moved up toward the 92nd floor.

"What?" said Remo.

"You are not permitted to kill this child," Chiun said.

Remo spun toward him. "What?"

"He is a child. His life is sacred in Sinanju," Chiun said. "A master cannot willingly take a child's life."

"That's Sinanju," said Remo. "This is New York."

"But you are a master. You are bound by the tradition."

"Bulldookey," said Remo. "You think I'm going to let this little sparkplug incinerate me, like Tungsten the Medium?"

"Tung-Si the Lesser," Chiun said. "Rules are rules."

"Good for you," Remo. "Don't go breaking any. And don't go giving any to me. This little swine killed Ruby, and I'm cancelling his library card."

The elevator door opened. Remo stepped out.

Chiun said "I'll stay here." He pressed the CLOSE DOOR button.

In the corridor, Remo paused and then heard the sound. It was a fast, crackling noise. He breathed deep, and the acrid smell of burning wood bit into his sensitive nostrils.

Remo ran along the carpeted floor, lifting his head like a dog scenting air. At an intersection of corridors, he moved toward the sound and smell of fire at the southeast corner of the building. He found the offices of the Safety First Grandslam Insurance Company. Through the frosted glass of the door, he could see the tongues of flames. The

168

Safety-First Grandslam Insurance Company. Where had he heard that name?

He pushed his way through the locked door. Sure. It was the company that had issued those life insurance policies that the Reverend Witherspool had hoped would make him rich.

The office was burning. Desks were afire, bookshelves were smoldering and, as Remo watched, smoke pouring from open file cabinets was turning red and then exploding into flame. A large computer ran the entire length of one wall. Smoke and flames shot from its opening like a slot machine paying off in fire.

Remo ignored the fires and pushed through the doors into all the connecting offices. Sparky was not there.

He came back out into the main office and looked at the burning computer. He remembered the policies written on those poor families in Newark. He looked at the fire extinguisher on the wall. He looked at the burning computer.

"Screw 'em," he said and walked out into the hall.

Where was the kid?

He ran along the corridors, pausing every so often to listen, but there were no more sounds—no crackle of flame, no whoosh of smoke, no breathing, no footsteps.

The kid had left the floor. Where had he gone?

Remo thought for a split second. He must have gone down. He might be trying to set fires all the way down to the bottom of the building. He would not have gone up because a fire on a lower floor might trap him up high. He must have gone down.

When he reached the elevators, the walls and the paint on the metal doors were burning. The carpet was ablaze, too. The kid had waited, trying to trap Remo on the burning 92nd floor. Remo ran back along the corridor, found an exit door, and ran down to the 91st floor. He pushed open the hallway door and listened. All was silent. No sound of human; no sound of fire.

He began to work his way down through the building. Ninetieth floor. Eighty-ninth. Eighty-eighth. The kid could be anywhere. There were more fires burning on the 80th floor and again on the 74th. Remo let the fires sizzle. That was for the fire department, assuming they were not on vacation in any month with more than 27 days in it. But there was no sign of Sparky.

Every floor. Checking all the way down.

Remo opened the door to the 67th floor.

As he did, he heard a voice call out, "Took you long enough, sucker."

The sound came from a corridor to his left, and Remo ran along it. At the end of the corridor, he looked right, then left. A door was open at one far end of the hall. He walked slowly toward it.

This was it.

Remo stepped into the office through the open door and saw Kid Blaze standing across the room, near a window.

He looked at Remo.

"Is Solly dead?"

"Just like you're going to be," Remo said.

The boy laughed.

"Why'd you set those fires upstairs?"

The youth shook his head. "They're nothing. Just to keep you interested."

"I knew they weren't big enough to mean anything."

"That's right. From here down, I take this building apart," Sparky said.

"To do that, you've got to get through this door behind me," Remo said.

"Then I'll just have to." The youth paused. He squinted across the room at Remo's face. "It seems like we've done this before," he said.

"You wouldn't know about it, but our ancestors did. A long time ago."

"Yeah? Who won then?"

"Your team," Remo said.

"I'll have to keep our record clean," the kid said. "First you. Then this building. Then who knows? I'm ready to move on to bigger things. Maybe the White House or Congress. The Pentagon. Who knows? All I know is I don't need Solly stopping me everytime I'm trying to have some fun."

"That woman you killed in Newark. Was that fun?"

"You betcha. And you're going to be fun. People in the street. Cats, dogs, passing cars. It's all fun."

"You're a freaking looney," Remo said. "Say good night, looney."

He started across the room, just as Sparky McGurl raised his arms. As Remo reached the row of desks in front of the youth, they flashed into flame. Through the flames, he could see the boy sizzling blue, flames crackling like electricity from his fingertips. The desks were incinerating in front of Remo's eyes. Great gouges of wood exploded into flame, popping up into the air, flying past Remo's head, and he backed off.

He felt heat behind him, and as he wheeled, he

171

saw the floor burning behind him. Flames were shooting up from the floor, straight up, like a wall, an upside-down waterfall of fire. And then the fire was on both sides of him, too. Floor, walls, desks, furniture—everything was ablaze.

Above the crackle of the flames came the high-pitched laugh of Sparky McGurl.

"You're done for. Say good night, sucker," he called out.

Remo felt the floor begin to weaken under his feet. The ring of fire around him grew in closer. Through the licking of the thick flames, he could see Sparky near the window, and with a sinking feeling, he saw that the boy was glowing even more intensely with the fire power. Remo's weight buckled slightly into the floor. It would be going soon. The flames were now spitting toward his skin; his bare arms felt the singe of heat from the awful ring of fire. He lowered his body temperature to withstand the blaze, but he knew it was drawing drastically down on his stores of energy. If he had a move to make, he'd have to make it now.

Remo coiled his legs into a crouch, then sprang upward, his pointed fingers thrust out in front of him like the business ends of tiny spears. He drove his fingers hard into the plasterboard of the ceiling. His fingers passed through the board and then grabbed onto the metal ceiling beam overhead. He gripped both hands around the metal beam, then swung himself out and through the ring of fire. He landed beyond the fire on the floor of the office.

Sparky growled his anger. He aimed his hands at Remo. Remo darted for the water cooler in the office, yanked off the giant bottle of water, and with

172

the side of his hand slashed off the neck of the bottle. He tossed the water at Sparky, just as the boy was aiming twin bolts of fire at Remo. Remo ducked below the racing flames. The water, all ten gallons of it, splashed on the boy. He sizzled. For a moment he vanished behind a cloud of steam. Remo could see his fire aura change almost immediately from hot yellow-white down through red and blue to human skin.

He stood there like a dog that had prowled the streets through a rainstorm, bedraggled and sad looking. It was easy now. Remo picked up a stone pen holder from a desk. Just toss it through the boy's skull, before he had a chance to recharge himself and start the blazes again.

He drew his arm back to throw the heavy weight at the boy, to deliver the killing blow. But he could not throw it. Slowly, he let his arm drop to his side. He shook his head. Chiun and his goddamn legends were going to get him killed one day. Throw the damn thing. But he couldn't.

If anyone ever needed killing, this vicious little animal, this twisted product of too many wrongs, this murderer of Ruby Gonzalez, deserved death— and Remo could not deliver it.

Sparky was screaming. "It won't save you," he yelled. "I'm not done yet." Remo could see the boy's face screwed up with the intensity of his effort to begin his eerie fire glow. Remo taunted him by beckoning to him with his hand.

"C'mon, twerp," Remo called. "Come and get me. Or is it only women and children you kill? Come on, nit."

Sparky was turning blue again. His internal fires

173

were regenerating themselves. "I'm going to wrap my hands around your neck," he yelled, "and hold on until they burn right through."

"What are you waiting for?" Remo said. "Come on." He lifted his chin. "Here's my neck, punk, you sicky little bastard. Come get it."

With a growl, even as his aura was changing from blue to the hotter red, Sparky raced at Remo. Remo waited until the boy was almost on him, until he could feel the heat from the kid's fingers. And then Remo ducked out of the way. The momentum of Sparky's charge carried him past Remo, into the circle of fire from which Remo had escaped, and the heaviness of his steps caused him to burst through the flaming floor. Remo turned to see the boy crash through the weakened floor down into the rooms below. Remo expected to hear the thump of his body hitting the floor. But there was no thump. There was only a squishing sound and then a pitiful, heart-rending scream that ended abruptly, as if the screamer had run out of air and could take no more breaths.

Remo carefully picked his way past the fire and looked down through the hole in the floor. Sparky McGurl had fallen so that the flat part of his body was impaled on a long wooden coat rack shaped like a spear, which was standing in the middle of the floor, directly below the hole in the floor. Standing next to the coat rack was Chiun. He look at Remo and held his arms out to his sides, saying only, "A terrible accident."

Then he turned to look at the boy, whose body had now reverted to human color, but whose look as he hung, impaled, was a dead, inhuman mixture of pain and panic.

174

"Some accident," Remo said.

"People have to be careful where they leave their clothes racks," Chiun said blandly.

CHAPTER SIXTEEN

The firemen's strike was settled by a compromise: those firemen who wanted to go deer hunting could have the first day of deer season as a vacation day; those who didn't could have St. Swithin's day off.

The fires were out around the city; the twin towers of the World Trade Center had been saved from serious damage except for the offices of the Safety First Grandslam Insurance Company, which were totally wrecked.

Remo and Chiun were back in their hotel room overlooking Central Park.

Remo was satisfied.

"We evened the score for Ruby," he said.

Chiun nodded. "Yes," he said. "You paid it back by death because this is your way, as it is my way. Have you finally realized you are an assassin, a dealer in death? When retribution is required, we do not write letters to the editor. We do not go on picket lines. We deal in a much more basic way with those who threaten the fabric of our civilized society. You must be an assassin because there is nothing else you can be. You cannot be a fisherman or a man who demonstrates on television machines that cut carrots. You have tried those things. You cannot do them. What you can do is what you have been trained to do. Be an assassin. Like me, you must kill to live."

Remo was lying on the couch. He looked out the window at the smokeless sky. "It's a shit deal, Chiun," he said.

"They are the cards that fate dealt you," Chiun said.

"I know," Remo said. "I know."

Later in the day, he asked Chiun for Ruby's medal.

"I threw it away," Chiun said. "It was cheap junk and it turns your neck green to wear it."

Remo looked at him in surprise. "You gave Ruby junk?" he asked.

"Would I do that?" asked Chiun.

Later that night, Smith came to their hotel room. He carried not only his gray briefcase, but a small box wrapped in manila paper.

Smith told Remo he had done good work with the two arsonists. "Even though it wasn't technically a CURE assignment," Smith said, "it was the proper thing to do."

"I'm glad you liked it," Remo said. "But I didn't do it for you or your dipshit organization."

"I know," Smith said. "For Ruby." He was silent a moment, then he added, "Remo, I regret what happened to her as much as you do. I really liked Ruby."

"But not enough that you wouldn't ask me to kill her," said Remo.

Smith nodded. "That's correct. I did not like her so much that I was going to jeopardize our organization and our country. You know that we live on secrecy, and if we're exposed, our whole government could go under."

"Somehow, Smitty," said Remo, "I just don't give a rat's ass."

Smith excused himself. He stopped at the door and, as an afterthought, tossed the manila-wrapped box to Remo. "The desk clerk asked me to give this to you." Then he left.

There was no return address on the package.

Remo opened it up. There was a metallic silver box inside. Printed in gold across the top of it was the legend: RUBY'S WIG EMPORIUM, NORFOLK, VA."

Remo looked at Chiun in confusion. Chiun's face was blank.

Remo opened the box. It contained a curly blond wig for a man, in a style made famous by professional wrestlers.

He lifted it out of the box as if it were a dead mouse, looked at it, and then looked back inside the box. There was a piece of paper under the wig.

He dropped the wig on the floor and opened the note.

It read, "This is for your pointy little head, turkey."

The note was unsigned, but in his mind, Remo could almost hear Ruby Gonzalez screaming at him across the distance.

He looked at Chiun and caught the old man in one of his rare smiles. Suddenly, he knew the truth. Ruby lived and Chiun knew that she lived.

Remo smiled.

"The medal?" he asked.

"A cheap copy she had made of the one I gave her. She was just waiting for a chance to drop it somewhere to prove her death." said Chiun. "When she found that body in the fire, that was her chance."

"She was the one who called you in St. Louis and told us to go to New York?" Remo said.

Chiun nodded. "Of course."

"And Smith?" Remo asked.

"He thinks that Ruby is dead," said Chiun.

"What should we do?" asked Remo.

"We should let sleeping lies lie," said Chiun. "What emperors don't know won't hurt their assassins."

The Destroyer
Warren Murphy